FOR ANNABELLE & AMELIE
TWUMASI-ANKRAH
- GPJ

FOR TIM & CHRIS, YOU KNOW WHY
- LF

STRIPES PUBLISHING LIMITED
An imprint of the Little Tiger Group
1 Coda Studios, 189 Munster Road,
London SW6 6AW

Imported into the EEA by Penguin Random House Ireland,
Morrison Chambers, 32 Nassau Street, Dublin D02 YH68

A paperback original
First published in Great Britain in 2022

Text copyright © Gareth P. Jones, 2022
Illustrations copyright © Louise Forshaw, 2022
ISBN: 978-1-78895-312-2

The right of Gareth P. Jones and Louise Forshaw to be identified as the
author and illustrator of this work respectively has been asserted by them in
accordance with the Copyright, Designs and Patents Act, 1988.

MIX
Paper from
responsible sources
FSC® C171272

The Forest Stewardship Council® (FSC®) is a global, not-for-profit organization dedicated to
the promotion of responsible forest management worldwide. FSC defines standards based
on agreed principles for responsible forest stewardship that are supported by environmen-
tal, social, and economic stakeholders. To learn more, visit www.fsc.org

2 4 6 8 10 9 7 5 3 1

SoLVE YOUR OWN MYSTERY

THE TIME THIEF

SOLVE YOUR OWN MYSTERY

The Time Thief

GARETH P. JONES

ILLUSTRATED BY LOUISE FORSHAW

LITTLE TIGER

LONDON

CLASSIFIEDS

Choose Mermail!

Send your mail by mermaid tail.

Ocean or river, we'll deliver!

Come browse in **Stonewater Books**

Spell books, Vampire Lore & Gnome Improvements

On The Rocks
The Sirens' Milkshake Bar

We'll sing for your supper!
(All drinks served on the rocks)

Time traveller seeks travelling companion

(Deadline for applications: the day before yesterday)

Witch Finders:

If you've lost something we'll help you find it – no matter where, what, how ... or witch

Call: 0848 MILKBIRD

EDWIN'S STUFF

THE TIME SPONGE

YOU GLANCE AT YOUR WATCH and wonder how much longer you'll have to wait for your boss to turn up. Since you started work as assistant to a private detective, you've got used to hanging around strange places. For the most part, Haventry is a very ordinary town but its shady side is populated by vampires, werewolves, ghosts, goblins and various other strange creatures of the night. Your boss, Klaus Solstaag, is a yeti. Working with him is usually pretty interesting but right now it's early in the morning, freezing cold and you're locked out of the office.

It's grey and miserable, the sky heavy with the threat of rain, so you're relieved when you hear the unmistakable sound of Klaus's car, Watson. The engine barks and snarls because, unlike most of the cars driving around the town, Watson used to be a dog. There was a time you would have considered that strange, but you've been working on the shady side long enough to understand that things are a little different here. Watson parks next to you, enthusiastically wagging his exhaust pipe.

The passenger door pops open.

"Morning," growls Klaus. "Get in."

You do as you're told. You're still fastening your seatbelt when Watson pulls away. An air freshener hangs from the rear-view mirror, but it isn't strong enough to mask your boss's distinctive aroma. He yawns and you cover your nose to avoid inhaling his morning breath. You wonder how long he's been awake. It's not unusual for him to spend the early hours trailing a suspect or chasing up a possible lead, but it's been a couple of months since your last big case.

A jingle plays on the radio.

"Oh yes! Oh no!
It's the Nick Grimm Show
On Shady Side Radio!"

"It's just coming up to eight thirty," says the DJ. "I'm Nick Grimm and now it's time to get more on today's big story..."

"Listen to this," says Klaus. "This is what we're working on."

The DJ continues, "Last night, a rare and valuable

exhibit was stolen from the Museum of Magical Objects and Precious Stones. The Unusual Police Force are investigating the theft of the Time Sponge. Here's time-travel expert and author Professor Timothy O'Leary explaining this object's powers..."

A higher-pitched voice says, "The Time Sponge is utterly unique. While ordinary sponges grow on the ocean bed and absorb water, this object was formed by the temporal tides and can absorb time itself. In other words, squeeze the sponge and everything freezes."

Klaus takes a sharp corner so fast that you have to grab the side of the seat. Watson yelps. He doesn't like being pinched. You wonder why Klaus is in such a hurry. You haven't seen him so wired since the case involving Dr Franklefink's missing Monster Maker.

On the radio, the DJ says, "Curator Doddwhistle, who has run the museum for over two centuries, is appealing for anyone with information to come forwards."

"We simply must get the sponge back," an elderly female voice says. "It was on loan from a very old friend of mine and the consequences of it falling into the wrong hands are unthinkable."

"For more on this story, we go over live to *News of the Unusual* reporter Gretchen Barfly-Sewer who is on the scene and, hopefully, on the line."

"Thanks, Nick," replies a rasping female voice. "Yesterday, I attended a press night at the museum, after three mermaids delivered the sponge to Haventry. Curator Doddwhistle was the host and the sparkling pop was flowing. Other guests included the academic, Professor O'Leary, and two senior members of the Unusual Police Force, who were on hand to oversee the sponge's security, all of whom must now surely be prime suspects in this mystery."

"And should we include your name on the suspect list, Gretchen?" asks Nick.

Gretchen lets out a burst of laughter that goes straight through you like a dagger. You've heard that a banshee screech can render humans helpless.

You're certainly relieved when she stops.

"I hardly think I'm a suspect, Nick," says Gretchen. "I personally witnessed Chief Inspector Darka lock the exhibit room with the Time Sponge inside when the press night finished. That was at ten o'clock. Darka says he checked the room at midnight and discovered that the sponge was gone."

"I see," says Nick Grimm. "I gather the sponge was to be featured as part of a new time-travel exhibition at the museum."

"It was the key exhibit," says Gretchen. "Also on display were the Memory Basin, which shows images of the past, the Occasional Lamp, which shifts between different time periods, and a bowl of Fortune Cookie Dough. But the Time Sponge was the only thing taken."

"Still. It must be a blow for the museum," interjects the DJ. "They haven't been doing so well recently, have they?"

"No. Curator Doddwhistle was hoping that her time-travel exhibition would help revive the museum's fortunes following recent money problems. Back when the snakes on the old gorgon's head could still turn people into stone, Doddwhistle had a fine collection of statues, but these days she's losing her sight and her museum is rapidly losing its appeal."

"It's certainly been a while since I visited," admits the DJ. "And wasn't there a rumour about the museum being turned into a shopping mall?"

"That's right," said Gretchen. "The recently elected Night Mayor Franklefink has made no secret of his ambitions to convert the old building. Unfortunately, Franklefink was unavailable for comment as he is currently on an official visit to Transylvania."

"Thanks, Gretchen," says the DJ. "We'll be keeping our listeners up to date with all the developments in this locked-room mystery, but right now, it's over to our weather witch, Chloe Cleverly."

A witch cackles then says, "After a clear night, there will be a rainy spell this morning. Then I'll do a sunny one around lunchtime. In the afternoon there will be a downpour of worms, which will be disgusting for most of us but nice weather for ducks..."

Klaus switches off the radio. "You and I are going to find the Time Sponge," he announces. "Business has been slow. Solving a high-profile crime like this could give us just the boost we need."

You've never known your boss to take a case

without being hired to do so. You wonder if there's something he isn't telling you. It wouldn't be the first time. Klaus often plays his cards close to his chest. You decide not to say anything at this stage and spend the rest of the journey jotting down details you picked up from the radio report.

By the time Klaus pulls up outside the museum, you've finished your list of subjects. It's an old, grubby building with ornate turrets and smeary windows. The sign outside reads: *MUSEUM OF MOPS*. Most people on the other side of town wouldn't dream of going inside such a drab-looking place but the residents of Haventry's Shady Side understand that there's rather more to it than meets the eye. A police officer is inspecting tyre marks running up the ramp that leads to the entrance. Hearing Watson's engine, she spins around and says, "Hey! You can't park there."

"Ah, morning, Elphina," Klaus responds breezily as he opens the car door and steps out. You follow his lead.

"It's Detective Sergeant Rigmarole to you," replies the officer, "and you must have a hairball in your ear, Solstaag. I said, *you cannot park there.*"

Klaus opens the trunk, pulls out a spare tyre and

lobs it down the road. "Fetch!" he yells.

With a happy rev of his engine, Watson sets off after the tyre. Cars swerve to avoid a collision as he snatches it up and zooms straight through a red light. Horns beep and drivers shout at him but Watson has already disappeared around a corner.

"Problem solved," says Klaus.

"Do you have any idea how many laws you've just

broken?" Rigmarole pulls out a pad and pen.

Klaus laughs. "So you've been promoted to detective sergeant? Congratulations."

"Yes, there've been quite a few changes since Darka threw you off the force."

"He didn't throw me off." Your boss sounds irritated. "I left the UPF."

Rigmarole turns to you. "Is that what he told you?"

Klaus rolls his eyes but Elphina continues. "I'll bet he never mentioned that Chief Darka gave him a choice: either start doing as he was told or leave."

Klaus has never spoken to you about his reasons for leaving the UPF, but what Rigmarole says doesn't surprise you. Your boss often goes about things in an unconventional way. He doesn't seem best pleased that Rigmarole has brought his dismissal up now. He changes the subject.

"Is it my imagination or have you grown, Elphina?"

"New stilts." Rigmarole opens her long coat and you see that she's actually an elf standing on a pair of stilts. She wiggles her leg. It rattles. "I'm still wearing them in," she says, "but don't worry, there isn't a thief in this town who could outrun me." Rigmarole tightens the straps of her stilts and buttons up her coat. "The new mayor wants this town cleaned up and I'm the one to get the job done. I'm moving up in the world, Klaus."

"Why? Are you planning on buying some even taller stilts?" Klaus chuckles.

"I should have you arrested for insulting an officer," says Rigmarole.

"Come on, I'm only teasing." Klaus grins. "I'm just here to take a look around. I heard about the Time

Sponge being stolen. I thought maybe I could help you find it."

"Sorry, I can't let you in." Rigmarole blocks his way. "This area is sealed off until the Ghoul Forensic team sweeps it for evidence. Besides, if anyone is going to solve this mystery, it's me."

"You?" snorts Klaus.

"You can laugh all you like. I'll prove I'm the best detective in this town."

Klaus gives her a hard stare but she doesn't flinch. "They said on the radio that the door was locked at the time of the theft," says Klaus. "Of course, when it comes to locked-room mysteries, nine times out of ten, it's the most obvious solution – the person with the key. So who had it last night?"

"Chief Darka was taking care of the security personally," said Rigmarole.

"Yes, but you were both at the party last night, knocking back the sparkling pop, I'll bet."

"I don't drink when I'm on duty," says Rigmarole.

"Surely the chief had a few glasses, though," says Klaus. "I remember what he's like once the sparkling pop is flowing."

You've seen Klaus use this technique before,

acting friendly in order to get his suspects to lower their guard. Rigmarole momentarily forgets herself and chuckles. "You can say that again. A few more glasses and he would have been singing that song about the bull in the china shop."

"I remember that one." Klaus guffaws. "What's it called again?"

"'Do the Smash!'"

They're both laughing now.

"So, what happened after the party?" asks Klaus.

"He kept watch inside the building. I was positioned out here."

"And I suppose he had the only key, did he?" asks Klaus casually.

"I think there's a spare in Doddwhistle's room but—"

"DS Rigmarole," growls a low, gravelly voice. "I hope you aren't conversing with a member of the public about a police matter." You feel a blast of warm air on your neck. Rigmarole gulps.

You turn to see an expanse of dark blue material making up the uniform of a police officer as tall and wide as your boss. He wears a cap and a pair of sunglasses. His beard is dark and dense. He looks nothing short of terrifying.

"Darka." Klaus offers his hand.

Chief Inspector Darka snorts. He removes his glasses, revealing his bullish red eyes. He steps under the police tape and you spot his tail. Chief Inspector Darka is a minotaur, and, right now, not a very happy one.

"You shouldn't be here, Klaus. You no longer work for the UPF," he says. "It's *our* job to find this sponge. Not yours. I have to answer directly to Night Mayor Franklefink on this one. Haven't you got a case you've been paid to investigate? A missing cat or something?"

"How do you know someone hasn't hired me to find the Time Sponge?" counters Klaus.

This strikes you as an interesting question. Klaus hasn't mentioned being hired to you. Is he bluffing? Or is there something he's holding back?

"Even if someone had hired you, this is UPF business. Sorry, Klaus." Chief Inspector Darka turns to Rigmarole. "See that no one goes in or out. No one."

He storms into the building.

"He's in quite a mood," says Klaus.

"Isn't he always? Do you remember that time when he—" Rigmarole catches herself. "You should go now, Klaus."

"See you round, Elphina."

You're relieved when Klaus turns to leave. He knows these UPF officers well but you don't much fancy being thrown in a cell. He walks fast. Seeing his nose twitch, you realize he's caught the whiff of something cooking. Klaus has a big appetite, which is hardly a surprise, given how huge he is.

Just up the road from the museum, a caravan is parked. The sign on the side reads: THE WITCHES' OVEN. The witches, Bridget and Burnella Milkbird, are sitting outside their food truck, sipping frothing liquid from silver goblets. Inside, their purple-haired monster Bootsy is washing up dishes. Klaus eagerly peruses the menu but you hesitate. You've encountered this pair of magical mischief-makers before, and their wand-waggling too often spells trouble as far you're concerned.

"If it isn't Klaus and his little human helper," says Burnella. "What are you after?"

"What have you got?" replies Klaus.

"Broth or steeeeeew," moans Bootsy.

"What's the difference?" asks Klaus.

"Broth … is … hot," he replies, taking his time over each word. "Stew … is … not."

"How about a couple of hot chocolates?" suggests Klaus.

You would like something to warm your hands on, but you're not sure how much you trust anything brewed by these witches.

"Hot chocolate for the yeti and his human pet. Coming up," says Bridget. "Get ready to catch."

"Mocca-chocca, loco CHAAA!" Burnella chants as she waggles her twig-like fingers.

You hold out your hands, unsure what's going to happen, and a steaming mug of hot chocolate materializes between your fingers. You flinch in surprise, sending hot brown liquid sloshing over the top and scalding your fingertips.

You blow on the steaming mug and your burnt fingers, but Klaus downs his drink in one. "How's the catering game, then?" he asks.

"It's not what it was," says Burnella. "We were thinking of trying out a new line of work."

"Like what?" asks Klaus.

"I don't know. Maybe we'll go into the detective business like you," she replies.

"Couldn't do any worse than you," says Bridget. "I'll bet you haven't got a clue who took this Time Sponge, have you?"

Klaus raises an inquisitive eyebrow. "What do you know about the Time Sponge?"

"Everyone knows about it. It's all over the newspapers." Burnella holds up a copy of *News of the Unusual*.

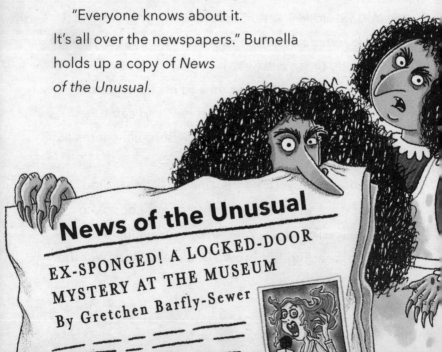

News of the Unusual

EX-SPONGED! A LOCKED-DOOR MYSTERY AT THE MUSEUM
By Gretchen Barfly-Sewer

"There's been a new edition since then," says Bridget, holding up another paper with the headline:

TIME THIEF STILL AT LARGE
BUT WHO TOOK THE SPONGE?

"I'm beginning to wonder if it was good idea selling her that magic printing press," says Burnella.

"It's a good story, though, this one. I reckon it was the mermaids," says Bridget. "They're a slippery lot. I'll bet they're up to something fishy."

Both witches burst out laughing.

Klaus scowls. "Funny as that is, it doesn't make sense. The mermaids delivered the sponge to Haventry. Why would they bring it here then steal it?"

"Well, they're not all there, are they, mermaids?" says Bridget. "They've got memories like goldfish. We never get anything sent by Mermail since those wands we ordered never turned up."

"Besides, they only brought the sponge here. It actually belongs to Bernard the time-bending lobster," says Burnella.

Klaus nods sagely. You have no idea what a time-bending lobster is but your boss doesn't seem surprised by this news. Once again, it occurs to you that he knows more than he's letting on.

"Thanks for the hot chocolate," says Klaus, handing over the money.

"Any time," replies Burnella. "Time. D'you get it? As in the Time Sponge."

"Honestly, Burnella, your jokes are older and stinkier than Bootsy's socks," says Bridget.

"Soccckkkks," repeats Bootsy.

"Come on," says Klaus. "Let's go. Mermail employees usually stay at Hotel Hostile, which is around the corner, so we could go there and talk to the mermaids." He pauses and thinks. "Or should we head back to the crime scene and try to take a sneaky look around before forensics arrive? It's your call."

? Do you want to talk to the mermaids?

Turn to page 46

TWO MERMAIDS AND A MAILMAN

? Or do you want to go to the crime scene?

Turn to page 29

GUARD-GOYLES

GUARD-GOYLES

"RIGMAROLE IS STILL WATCHING THE front door so we'd better try the back," says Klaus.

You follow him down an alley lined with overflowing bins, feeling your heartbeat quicken. Chief Inspector Darka isn't the sort of person you want to upset, and yet here you are going against his strict orders to stay away from the crime scene.

The alley leads to the back entrance of the museum. There are a few stone steps leading up to a door. Klaus approaches but a nasal voice calls from above.

"Not so fast, you."

You look up. The ugliest gargoyle you've ever

seen perches on the corner of the building at an angle that means he can only just see you out of the corner of his eye.

"Who said that? Is that you, Spitz?" says another, equally nasal, voice. You spot a second gargoyle on the other corner of the building. He also tries to peer around to look at you.

"Of course it's Spitz, Granite. Who else do you think is up here?" says the first gargoyle.

"I don't know. I never actually see you, do I? I thought you'd gone on holiday."

"Gone on holiday?" exclaims Spitz. "You thought I'd packed my bags, booked a hotel and *GONE ON HOLIDAY*! You don't think that having a RUDDY GREAT BIG BUILDING attached to my rear end would cause a few problems with that?"

"If you've been here, why have I been playing I-spy with a pigeon for the past week?"

"Because we've been stuck in the same place for two hundred and twenty-six years, two months, five

days, three hours and
fifteen minutes.
What's left to
spy?"

Granite
considers this for a
moment. "Pigeons?"

"You see what I
have to put up with?"
exclaims Spitz. "Stuck up
here with nothing to do but
listen to him saying, 'I spy
with my little eye something beginning with P.'"

"Fascinating as this is," says Klaus, "I'm more
interested in last night's robbery."

"Oh, I know all about that," says Spitz. "I'm just
above Curator Doddwhistle's window. She's furious.
She's been on the phone to the insurance company
all morning."

Klaus looks at you. "If Doddwhistle is insured
against theft, she could be due a pay-out."

You make a note of this. Next to Curator
Doddwhistle's name, you write *insurance money* and
possible motive.

"I understand it went missing between ten and

midnight," says Klaus. "Who was in the building then?"

"Curator Doddwhistle definitely was," says Spitz. "She hardly ever leaves. Her bedroom is next to her office."

"And Chief Inspector Darka was guarding the exhibit room," says Granite. "I'd recognize his heavy breathing anywhere."

"Did he leave his position at any point?" asks Klaus.

"Just before midnight I heard footsteps and a toilet flush," says Granite, "so I guess he had to spend a penny."

"And now you mention it, I think I did hear the back door open and close at some point," says Spitz.

"Do you have a time?" asks Klaus.

"Do we look like we wear watches?" snaps Spitz. "But I know it was after midnight that someone used the door because I'd already heard the grandfather clock chime."

"Any idea who would have been sneaking around so late?" asks Klaus.

"No," admits Spitz. "We're not very well angled."

"And most people use the front door to the museum," says Granite. "Except for that horrible

Gretchen Barfly-Sewer. She always sneaks in and out the back way."

"I thought you couldn't see who uses the door," said Klaus.

"We can't but Gretchen usually yells something insulting at us," says Spitz.

"She called me a monstrous stone appendage once," says Granite.

"She said I was a glorified waterspout," adds Spitz.

"And that laugh of hers. It goes right through you." Granite shudders, creating a small shower of pebbles and dust.

Klaus checks that you're writing all this down. He's good at gathering information, but he needs your help to make sense of it all. As always, there's a lot to take in and it's hard at this stage to separate the vital clues from the irrelevant details.

"Anyway, the building is on lockdown. Darka said no one's allowed in," says Granite. "Especially no humans like this one."

You realize Granite is talking about you. It's not the first time someone on the Shady Side has viewed you with suspicion. You're grateful for the friendly pat on the back from Klaus, even if it does take your breath away.

"This one's with me," he says. "And seeing as you two are stuck there, I'm guessing there's not much you can do to stop us walking in."

He steps up and shoulders the door open. In spite of the protests from above, you follow him inside.

"So," he says. "Shall we go upstairs to speak to Curator Doddwhistle or stay down here and check out the crime scene?"

? Should you go and see Curator Doddwhistle?
Turn to page 35

THE GORGON AND THE SPARE KEY

? Or should you go and check out the display room?
Turn to page 55

TIME CRIME SCENE

THE GORGON AND THE SPARE KEY

YOU FOLLOW KLAUS UP THE dark staircase. The windows all have wooden shutters and the only light comes from small buzzing creatures trapped in large antique jars. You inspect one as you pass. It's the size of a fly but human in form with wings beating so fast they're invisible. Each one of these tiny people glows like a firefly. You're so fascinated by them that you forget where you are for a moment, until you feel Klaus's large hairy hand on your shoulder.

"Stay focused," he whispers. "Chief Inspector Darka is downstairs. If he finds us sneaking around, he won't just throw us out. He'll most likely arrest us. Me and him have stayed on good terms but I don't think he's ever forgiven me for leaving the UPF. He asks me to come back pretty much every time we speak, but now I'm freelance, there's nothing to stop him locking us both up."

You reach the top of the stairs, where you follow a winding corridor to a door with a sign that reads:

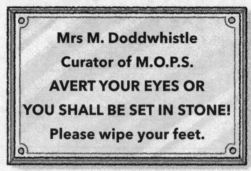

Mrs M. Doddwhistle
Curator of M.O.P.S.
AVERT YOUR EYES OR
YOU SHALL BE SET IN STONE!
Please wipe your feet.

Klaus whispers, "I've met Doddwhistle before but it's been a while, and her eyesight is pretty bad so I'm hoping she won't recognize me. That'll make this easier. The chances are, Chief Darka's instructed her not to talk to anyone about the theft."

Klaus knocks on the door.

"Enter," calls a voice.

Klaus places his hand on the handle but pauses before turning it. "You seem nervous," he says.

He's right. You've just noticed it isn't a handle he's gripping but what appears to be a stone hand attached to the door.

"Don't worry," says Klaus. "Doddwhistle hasn't turned anyone to stone for years."

He's trying to sound comforting but you can't help thinking about that hand and whoever it once belonged to.

"Well? Come in, then," calls Curator Doddwhistle irritably.

With some trepidation, you follow Klaus into the gloomy room. The shelves are full of old books, strange statues and rare artefacts. The heavy curtains are closed. The curator sitting behind the desk isn't quite the snake-haired demon you feared. She wears a patterned cardigan and a woollen hat. She's knitting.

"Hello, are you here to fix my computer?" She squints at you through the thick lenses in her glasses. "It's been on the blink all day."

Klaus glances at you and winks. "Yes, we are."

"Oh, good. It won't print... Or allow me to type anything... Or even turn on, now I come to think about it. And I need to have a look at the museum accounts. This closure is no good for business, no good at all." She shakes her head.

Klaus slips into character as an IT expert, speaking in a nasal voice. "We'll get your computer sorted out, madam. Perhaps if I could take a look..."

"Of course." Curator Doddwhistle stands up and shuffles across the room. She settles in a rocking chair with her knitting. You wonder if she meant to choose so many mismatched colours and what exactly it is she's knitting.

Klaus bends down behind her desk, pretending to take a look at the computer, but you can see him scanning the desk for clues. You're doing the same but are also aware of Curator Doddwhistle's eyes. She keeps looking up from her knitting to scrutinize you. You can't help but notice that her bobble hat keeps shifting, wriggling and letting out the occasional hiss.

"Why are there two of you?" she asks.

"This is my apprentice," says Klaus.

"I see. So long as there's nothing untoward.

You see, I have to be careful. We had a burglary last night."

"Ah, so that's what the UPF are doing here," says Klaus casually.

"For all the good it will do." Curator Doddwhistle sighs. "Chief Inspector Darka was overseeing the security himself when the Time Sponge was stolen. Useless. I knew I should have gone with that private security firm."

"Don't you have insurance to cover the theft?"

Klaus is fishing for information and Curator Doddwhistle takes the bait.

"I would if I hadn't fallen behind with the payments."

Once again, you're impressed with your boss's ability to extract information from suspects simply by chatting to them.

"I feel so terrible. This exhibition was supposed to revive our community's interest in the museum and the Time Sponge was the key exhibit. Bernard won't be happy when he finds out, either."

Klaus fiddles with the computer then casually asks, "Bernard?"

"Bernard the time-bending lobster," replies Doddwhistle. "He's an old friend. When I met him

I actually saved his life. He was involved with a seafood restaurant and had got himself in a bit of hot water at the time, you see." She chuckles. "He owed me a favour, which is how I convinced him to lend his Time Sponge to the museum."

"So it was your idea to include it?" asks Klaus.

"Well, no. Professor O'Leary told me I needed it. He's the real expert with all this timey-wimey stuff and he's right. We were booked solid for the first week with people keen to see the Time Sponge up close."

"Did Professor O'Leary contact the lobster?"

"No, that was me. He's very hard to get hold of because he spends his life swimming through the tides of time, which move back and forth between the past, the present and the future."

Klaus raises an eyebrow. "I don't really know what that means."

You know how he feels. You're struggling to keep up.

"Well, that's time travel for you," says Doddwhistle. "All I know is that the Time Sponge was the biggest draw and without it we have nothing."

"How did you get in touch with Bernard to arrange borrowing the Time Sponge?"

"He contacted me from the future, remembering I'd asked him around now. Like I say, it's all terribly confusing."

"It certainly is," says Klaus, catching your eye. "Make sure you're keeping notes on what we're doing here." He taps the keyboard, pretending he's talking about the computer. You don't need telling. You've been scribbling away throughout, making sure you're keeping track of all this information.

"Are you having any luck with that thing?" asks the curator.

"I'm still identifying all the possible reasons for the problem," says Klaus.

Again, he isn't talking about the computer, but the case.

"So, Professor O'Leary knew about the sponge, the mermaids brought it, Chief Inspector Darka and Detective Sergeant Rigmarole were looking after it and Gretchen Barfly-Sewer was reporting on it. Did anyone else visit the museum yesterday?"

The elderly curator pauses. "You seem very inquisitive for an IT person. You're not a reporter too, are you?"

Klaus laughs. "No. Unlike Gretchen, I have an interest in the truth."

"Well, yes. With that magical printing press of hers, she's an absolute menace. It wouldn't surprise me if she stole the sponge just to bump up her readership," says Curator Doddwhistle. "She certainly seems to be enjoying all this. She's brought out three more editions of the paper already." You spot several copies of the *News of the Unusual* on her desk. Two have the same headlines as the papers the witches showed you, but the other editions read:

"WE NEED MORE TIME TO CATCH THE THIEF," BEGS CHIEF DARKA

"SERIOUSLY. GO AWAY. I'M TOO BUSY FOR THIS," SAYS DESPERATE DARKA

"WILL YOU PLEASE STOP USING MY QUOTES AS HEADLINES?" PLEADS FAILING POLICE CHIEF

You hear a hiss from the top of Curator Doddwhistle's head. You've been told to avoid looking directly into a gorgon's eyes so you glance away and notice a row of large keys on one wall.

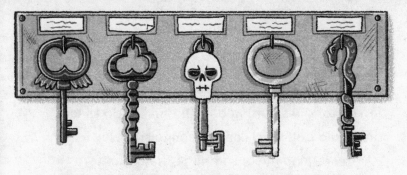

They all hang facing the same direction, except for the one labelled *MAIN EXHIBIT ROOM*. This one is turned the other way. You consider what this might mean. It could be nothing, or perhaps it's a sign that whoever hung the key there was in a hurry.

"It's all a game to that reporter," says Doddwhistle. "This museum has been a keystone of the community for hundreds of years but no one cares about history any more. No one cares about culture. Night Mayor Franklefink would rather turn the whole place into a shopping mall. A shopping mall! I need this exhibition to be a success to prove him wrong, but Darka's shut the whole thing down while he investigates."

"I can see that must be hard."

Up until this point, Klaus has stayed in character as an IT worker, but he speaks in his own voice as he shows genuine sympathy. You aren't the only one to notice. Curator Doddwhistle sits upright, puts her knitting down and removes her woollen hat. A nest of slithering snakes lies curled up on her head. They stretch out as they're released, hissing, their little forked tongues darting out. The snakes do all look rather old but it's still an unnerving sight.

"You remind me of someone," says Curator Doddwhistle slowly.

Klaus disguises his voice again, but you can tell he's concerned she's going to recognize him. "Like I say, we're the IT support, and you'll be pleased to know I've found the problem." Klaus is holding a plug in his hand. "This needs to go in the socket."

He plugs the computer in, presses the ON button and it flickers to life.

"So we'd better go to the next job. There's a troll down the road who's been struggling to access the internet."

Both of you leave before Curator Doddwhistle – and her snakes – can get a good look at you. You're pleased to be out of her office, but you feel a little stiff as you walk away. You haven't been turned to stone but you do wonder if your bones feel a little heavier than before.

You follow Klaus down the stairs, keen to get away, but he pauses when he hears voices.

"Morning, Susie."

"Morning, Bill. This room, is it?"

"Yes, that's the one."

Klaus pokes his head around the corner.

"Blast. It's the Ghoul Forensic team," he says. "They've come to check the area for evidence. We'll have to leave the crime scene for later."

You follow him out of the building into the grey, drizzly day. He keeps out of the gargoyles' sight as he makes his way back to the car.

"So what next? It was interesting what Doddwhistle said about Professor O'Leary requesting the sponge. Maybe we should have a word with him. Or should we be paying a visit to the reporter, Gretchen Barfly-Sewer? Doddwhistle is right. She's certainly going to town on reporting this."

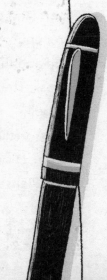

? Do you want to visit Professor O'Leary?

Turn to page 62

THE LEPRECHAUN LECTURER

? Or do you want to talk to Gretchen Barfly-Sewer?

Turn to page 70

THE BANSHEE REPORTER

TWO MERMAIDS AND A MAILMAN

HOTEL HOSTILE DOES NOT APPEAR in any of the guides to Haventry's most desirable places to stay. Looking at it from the outside, you'd be forgiven for thinking that it shut down a long time ago. Most of the windows are boarded up. The curtains are torn and mouldy. As Klaus opens the door into the reception area, you notice the wallpaper is peeling off and there are scratch marks all over the front desk. There's no one to greet you so Klaus rings a bell.

A cuckoo clock on the wall behind the desk clicks into action and a tiny wooden cuckoo pops out.

"Please don't ring the bell," says the cuckoo

before returning to
its clock.

Klaus rings the
bell a second time.

The cuckoo
reappears. "I said,
*please don't ring the
bell*. It's very annoying."

Klaus sighs but you
smile. The fact that even the clocks can answer
back on the Shady Side of Haventry is one of
the things you love about this job.

"Yes, but we—" Before Klaus can finish his
sentence the cuckoo is back inside the clock.

He rings the bell again. This time, when the
cuckoo emerges, Klaus grabs its beak. It can't
return to the clock but nor can it speak.

"Mmm-grmm-ggnmm," mumbles the cuckoo.

"I'm here to see the mermaids," says Klaus.
"Tell me where to find them and I won't have to
keep ringing the bell, will I?"

"Mmm-sswmmg mmm," says the cuckoo.

Klaus releases it.

The cuckoo gives a disgruntled little shake of
its wooden wings. "They're downstairs in the pool.

Awful guests. Noisy, messy eaters and they tip in mussels. Apparently *mermaids don't carry money*. Anyway, if you don't mind, I'm on the clock here. Please don't ring that bell again."

The cuckoo vanishes. Klaus shrugs, then finds a door marked *POOL*. There are three wheelchairs folded up by the side. You follow Klaus down the stairs. The smell of chlorine is overpowering. Voices echo off the tiled walls. You had expected mermaid song to sound hypnotic and soothing but the voice you hear is deep and coarse.

"Jimmy was a merboy
Who liked to suck his thumb
But when he was a naughty boy
His mum would slap his—"

Klaus pushes open a door and you see three mermaids. They're not how you imagined them.

The two female ones are splashing about in the pool but there are no colourful clam shell bikinis or long flowing locks. Instead they have garishly coloured hair poking out from under navy-blue swimming caps and they wear swimsuits with a logo made up of two Ms. The third mermaid is male and sits on the poolside, dangling his tail into the water. He wears a matching swimsuit but has removed his cap to reveal a bald head above a bushy black beard and a very hairy chest.

"You interrupted my song," he says.

"Yes, and Fred's very sensitive once he starts singing. Isn't that right, Amelie?" says the mermaid with purple hair.

"Isn't what right, Annabelle?" replies the one with green hair.

"Er. I'm not sure," admits Amelie. She turns to address you and Klaus. "Hey, are you from room service?"

"About time too," says Annabelle.

"Yeah. Where are our chips?" says Fred.

"They're on their way," replies Klaus, as quick as a flash. "Say, I've never met a male mermaid before."

"I'm a male mermaid mailman. What of it?"

"I meant no offence," adds Klaus quickly.

"Don't mind Fred," says Annabelle. "He's always grouchy when he's hungry. So about those chips..."

"What chips?" says Amelie.

"Yes, let's order some chips," says Fred.

"We *have* ordered them," says Annabelle.

"Ordered what?" asks Amelie.

"I'm not sure," admits Annabelle.

Fred turns to you. "Who are you, then? The chip chef?"

You exchange a bewildered glance with Klaus. "We'd like to ask you some questions."

"About chips?" asks Fred.

The three mermaids are definitely amusing but you are also a bit confused about what is going on.

"Are you feeling all right?" asks Klaus.

Annabelle says, "Show him the card."

"Oh yes, the card," replies Amelie. She grabs a dressing gown hanging by the side of the pool and pulls out a card, which she hands to you. It's a bit soggy and the writing is smudged, but it's readable.

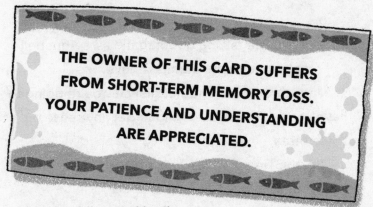

THE OWNER OF THIS CARD SUFFERS FROM SHORT-TERM MEMORY LOSS. YOUR PATIENCE AND UNDERSTANDING ARE APPRECIATED.

You hand the card back.

"We have a couple of questions about the Time Sponge," says Klaus.

All three mermaids flop back into the pool, making an enormous splash and sending water everywhere.

"Ah yes, I do remember that," says Annabelle, breaking the surface. "We delivered it to the museum yesterday. We're supposed to stay here until the exhibition is over, then take it back."

"We thought we'd do some shopping while we're in town," says Fred.

"It's so expensive here, though," says Amelie. "Back home, we always pay in clams and mussels."

"That's true but the shops back home mostly sell clams and mussels," adds Annabelle.

"Where's home?" asks Klaus.

"Atlantis," says Amelie. "Where the depot is."

"Why are we talking about that?" asks Annabelle.

"I can't remember," admits Amelie.

Klaus throws you another glance. You're going to have your work cut out trying to get any sense out of these three.

"So, the Time Sponge," says Klaus. "I understand you were employed to deliver it."

"That's right. Bernie hired us," says Annabelle.

"The time-bending lobster," adds Amelie.

"I remember him," says Fred. "He's the selfish one, right?"

"He's not selfish," says Annabelle. "He's a *shellfish*."

"Oh yeah. What did I say?" asks Fred.

"I can't remember," admits Annabelle.

"Yes, so the Time Sponge…" Klaus is losing patience and you know exactly how he feels.

"We don't have that," says Amelie. "We handed it over to the gorgon."

"Curator Doddwhistle," says Klaus.

"Yes, and there was a little green-haired fellow with her too," says Annabelle. "He seemed very interested in it. He snatched that sponge right out of our hands."

"Professor O'Leary," says Klaus.

"That's the one," says Annabelle.

"What's one what?" asks Fred.

"I'm not sure," admits Annabelle.

"Oh well, thoughts drift away but they usually swim back again eventually," says Amelie.

With another splash, Annabelle and Fred disappear under the water.

"I think we've got all we can out of this interview," Klaus says to you.

"Don't forget our ... what did we ask for again?" asks Amelie.

"You wanted chips," says Klaus.

Fred breaks the surface. "Did someone say chips?" he asks.

Klaus opens the door for you. Your socks squelch inside your damp shoes as you take the stairs back to the reception area. On his way out, Klaus shouts to the cuckoo clock, "Thanks for your help."

A muffled voice from inside replies, "Thanks for not ringing the bell."

Standing outside, Klaus says, "So? We could go find Professor O'Leary. He's based at Shady Side University, so we could pay him a visit and see why he was so interested in the sponge, or while we're on this side of town we could see if we can sneak into the museum now and take a look. What do you think? Should we sound out the next suspect or check out the scene of the crime? it's your call."

? Should you go back to the crime scene?
Turn to page 29
GUARD-GOYLES

? Or do you want to go see Professor O'Leary?
Turn to page 62
THE LEPRECHAUN LECTURER

TIME CRIME SCENE

"TREAD QUIETLY," SAYS KLAUS. "THIS museum is old and these floorboards squeak more than a barrel of overexcited mice."

You do as you're told, silently following your boss along the corridor, past oil paintings of strange-looking beasts and unnatural beings. A grandfather clock ticks loudly outside the exhibit room. The door is open but police tape blocks the way. Klaus pauses and points to a mirror on the opposite wall, reflecting the inside of the room.

CRIME SCENE – DO NOT ENTER

Inspector Darka stands with his back to you. He's in front of a plinth in the centre of the room. He's studying it closely, though you can't tell why. Once he's finished, he turns around and you see his large, bullish face. Klaus taps you on the shoulder. You have to move quickly. You scuttle back down the corridor and around a corner, just in time to avoid being seen. Thankfully, Darka walks in the other direction, towards the front door.

You hear him speaking into his radio. "Send in the forensic ghouls," he says.

"Will do, sir," replies DS Rigmarole through the radio.

The door slams.

"He's gone," says Klaus. "We don't have much time. The forensics team will be here to search for evidence in a matter of minutes."

You both move swiftly back to the display room. Klaus has to stoop low to get under the police tape but you only have to duck your head. Inside, you can see all the objects that make up the museum's time-travel exhibition.

There's a bowl of a grey gooey substance. It reminds you of cake mix but the label explains what it really is.

> ### FORTUNE COOKIE DOUGH
> *Stir the bowl then wait ten seconds.*
> *The fortune dough has awoken.*
> *A future truth you have beckoned,*
> *so read the words that will be spoken.*

"Try to avoid touching anything," warns Klaus, seeing the look in your eyes. The exhibits all look so intriguing, but this is a crime scene and you have to avoid tampering with it.

Across the room from the dough is the Occasional Lamp. It looks like an ordinary lamp except that it keeps vanishing, then reappearing a few seconds later. You would suspect it of being a hologram if it wasn't for its long black shadow. The sign reads:

> ### THE OCCASIONAL LAMP
> *This lamp exists in several timelines, endlessly travelling back in time then forward to every version of the future. It uses a 40-watt bulb. Please mind the wire.*

On the other side of the room is a basin, complete with taps and mirror but not plumbed in. A label on the wall reads:

THE MEMORY BASIN

Touch the water to see what has been.
The ripples of the past are there to be seen.
Then please wash your hands. It's good to be clean!

You know your mind should be on the job but you can't help yourself. You spend your working days trying to unpick the truth about the past and here, right in front of you, is an opportunity to gaze directly at events which have already taken place. You lean over and peer into the water. At first, it looks perfectly ordinary but, as you stare, the water begins to swirl. You feel your hand drawn to it. You dip the tips of your fingers in and an image appears.

It's the same room you're standing in, only it's full of people. You can see a little old lady in a cardigan and a wool hat talking to Inspector Darka. You can't hear them but you see him mouth the words, "Curator Doddwhistle". Also in the room is a woman with an ashen white face and a shock of red hair. She holds a small recording device as she interviews a short man in a green hat. She must be the reporter you heard on the radio. You guess that he's the expert in time travel, Professor O'Leary. They're both staring at the Time Sponge.

The waters shift and the scene vanishes but this is not the end of the vision. Now you see the outside of the museum. It's dark and there's only one person. Klaus is looking up at the building with a torch in his hand. He is alone.

You're not sure what this vision means. You turn around to check if the present Klaus is watching you.

He never mentioned coming to the museum before he picked you up this morning. You want to see if there's more, but when you look back at the basin, the vision has gone.

"Anything over there?" asks Klaus.

You shake your head.

"Not much here either," he says.

You join him by the plinth. On top of it is a small velvet cushion. You can see the slight dip where the sponge once rested. Taking a closer look, you notice a single strand of hair under the cushion. It's white, the same colour as your boss's.

A door creaks.

"Uh-oh, that must be the ghoul forensics," says Klaus. "We need to get out of here."

You quickly follow him out of the room and down the corridor. Voices approach from the front of the building.

"Morning, Susie."

"Morning, Bill. This room, is it?"

"Yes, that's the one."

You slip out of the building, moving swiftly away before the gargoyles start shouting again. Once you're clear, Klaus stops.

"Well, I'm not sure what we learned from that.

I didn't spot anything. But we can't go near the place again until the forensics team have gone."

You're still thinking about the images you saw in the basin. A part of you wants to ask Klaus outright, but he is your boss. You trust him. Besides, he wasn't the only one you saw. Professor O'Leary and Gretchen Barfly-Sewer were both staring at the Time Sponge in a way that made you suspicious. You wonder if the basin is trying to tell you something.

Klaus looks at you, smiles and says, "You look like you've seen a ghost."

You wish you had. You'd rather that than discover your boss has been lying to you. You decide not to say anything at this stage and focus on one of the other two suspects you saw in the basin ... but which one?

? "I think we should go and see the professor."
Turn to page 62
THE LEPRECHAUN LECTURER

? "I think we should talk to the reporter."
Turn to page 70
THE BANSHEE REPORTER

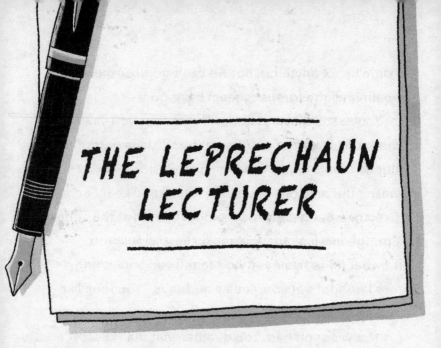

THE LEPRECHAUN LECTURER

SHADY SIDE UNIVERSITY IS AN impressive redbrick
building on the far side of town, around the back
of a fishfinger factory. The overpowering smell
lingers as you step out of the drizzle into the atrium.
Students and academics bustle around and you can
hear a voice from inside the main hall.

"That's O'Leary," says Klaus. "Churning out his
usual stuff on time travel, no doubt."

You pause before entering and peer through the
small window in the door. The circular lecture hall
is full. Every part of the Shady Side community is
represented: there are werewolves, vampires, ghosts
and goblins, all sitting quietly listening to a tiny

man with a goatee beard and bushy eyebrows and wearing a large green hat.

"Professor O'Leary is a leprechaun," says Klaus, "but don't bring up pots of gold or rainbows. He's a little sensitive about that stuff. Leave the talking to me."

You always do. It's what he's good at. Your strength lies in your ability to listen and observe. It's what makes you a good team. Your boss is the mouth of the operation. You are the ears.

As the lecture draws to a close, you hear the professor speaking with a soft Irish lilt. "As I said in my bestselling books, *A History of the Future* and *The Future of the Past*, time is neither a force nor a rule. Time is a suggestion. It is a map rather than a route." He pauses to allow himself an appreciative smile at his own words, then adds, "And talking of time, we are all out, so until next week, goodbye. Oh, and if you haven't already bought a copy of my books then they're available in—"

The rest of his sentence is lost under the sound of students noisily getting to their feet and leaving the hall. You hear some of them talking as they pass.

"He's so inspirational," says a drifting ghost student.

63

"Oh, come on. He only ever quotes from those two books. He hasn't had an original thought in years," moans a teenage zombie.

"I heard he had writer's block," adds a young vampire.

The students file out of the theatre as you and Klaus descend the stairs, moving against the flow. Professor O'Leary stands at the lectern tidying up his papers.

"Professor," says Klaus.

He turns around and smiles broadly. "Ah, Klaus, top of the morning to you. Who's your friend here?" He turns to you.

"This is my assistant. We're here on a case. We're looking for the Time Sponge."

"Oh, to be sure, the Time Sponge," says the professor. "I would have thought that would be a case for the UPF, would it not? You're not back working for them, are you?"

"No chance," replies Klaus. "I've done my time on the force."

"Ah well, I'm sure that old bull Darka would like to have you back. I think this one may be beyond their capabilities."

"Why would you think that?"

"Because whoever holds the Time Sponge can halt time, so he can." O'Leary demonstrates by freezing for a moment before giggling and continuing. "So if you ever get close to your thief, he could squeeze it and get away."

"Interesting that you should say *he*."

"It could be a she," Professor O'Leary adds quickly. "Or a they. Or maybe an it. I feel partly responsible, though."

"Partly responsible for taking it?" asks Klaus.

"Ha, no, not at all. I mean, I was the one who suggested it for the exhibition."

"Right. And I understand that you were there yesterday for the press night," says Klaus.

Professor O'Leary picks up a green fountain pen from the lectern and drops it into his bag. "I had to examine the sponge and verify it was the real thing. I did a brief demonstration of its powers."

"So you've actually squeezed it?"

"Only for the briefest of moments, yes," says O'Leary. "It's a fascinating object. When it contracts, it absorbs time and pauses the forward temporal flow."

"In English, please."

"Oh, I see. Put simply, when you squeeze it, time stops for everyone except for the sponge-wielder. The harder the squeeze, the longer the pause. When I tested it, I gave it a little squish and halted time for a couple of seconds. But a good hard squeeze could last a couple of hours, maybe a whole day."

"It sounds incredible."

"It is," admits Professor O'Leary. "To see a moment frozen in time like that. It takes your breath away."

"So you had access to the sponge and you have an interest in its powers. I know we're old friends but I'd be lying if I said you weren't on my list of suspects, professor."

"Me?" squeaks Professor O'Leary. "Why would I steal the Time Sponge?"

"You tell me." Klaus is goading him.

"Never mind accusing me," says Professor O'Leary. "I read in the latest edition of the *News of the Unusual* that you were spotted poking around the museum last night."

You glance at your boss. He doesn't look happy. You wonder if he's rattled because Gretchen is lying. Or maybe it's because she's telling the truth.

"This isn't about me," Klaus replies.

"It's not about me either." Professor O'Leary snaps his briefcase closed. "I'm sorry, but I have to go. If you really want to find out about the Time Sponge, perhaps you should learn a bit more about its owner."

"You mean Bernard the time-bending lobster?"

"Yes. He's connected to the sponge in ways

you couldn't begin to fathom. It's all in his autobiography," says Professor O'Leary. "I read it once. Very interesting but quite hard to follow as it keeps switching between the past, present and future tense. Time travellers don't make the best writers."

"Would I find a copy in Stonewater Books?"

"No, it was a limited edition, but there's a copy in the library. I have a couple of tutorials then I'm popping over. I could meet you there in an hour and show you."

"Thanks," says Klaus. "That might be useful."

"Well, then. Maybe I'll be seeing you later." The professor leaves.

Klaus waits until he's out of earshot before turning to you.

"He's still on my list but at least he's offering to help out. So what first? I think we should pay Gretchen Barfly-Sewer a visit. She always knows more than most. And while facts have never been her strong point, she might be able to shed some light, I suppose."

Klaus turns to you.

"What do you think? Time to visit the offices of the Haventry *News of the Unusual*?"

? Do you agree that it's time to speak to Gretchen?

Turn to page 70
THE BANSHEE REPORTER

? Or maybe you'd like to know whether Klaus really was spotted around the museum last night. In which case, it's time to ask him what he's hiding from you.

Turn to page 77
ACCUSING KLAUS

THE BANSHEE REPORTER

THERE ARE TWO LOCAL NEWSPAPERS covering daily events in Haventry. Most of the town's newsagents stock the *Haventry Chronicle,* which includes stories about potholes, roadworks and local council decisions.

The *Haventry News of the Unusual* covers the stories that affect the Shady Side of town. The newsroom is located above a milkshake bar run by sirens called On the Rocks. When you arrive outside, there's music blasting out. You peer through the window and see that the waitresses are singing about all the flavours of milkshake. "We have chocolate or lemon, fudge cake or melon, strawberry or kiwi, banana or raspberry."

"Mmm," says Klaus. "Sounds good to me. Maybe we should pop in and try one."

You're about to agree, but you bite your lip and resist the urge. You have a job to do. You point to the metal steps leading up to the *News of the Unusual* office door.

Klaus blinks and smiles. "Sorry. I find this place hard to resist but you're right. I'm pretty sure I've lost entire days in there trying to decide what flavours to have."

It's not easy to walk past the shop. The waitresses sing louder. "So many milkshakes, gloopy sweet, why not give yourself a treat?" You can still hear them as you walk into the newsroom.

Sitting behind a desk by the grubby window is a reporter with a mass of blood-red hair. She bangs her heel on the floor.

"Keep it down, you lot. Some of us are trying to work here while you sit around luring people. What is it with sirens and luring?"

She looks up at you and winks. There's a flicker of fire in her eyes. A shiver runs down your back. You're used to encountering all sorts of people in this job but Gretchen is a more intimidating figure than most.

"Ah, Klaus Solstaag," she says. "Once one of

the Unusual Police Force's most promising young officers. Now a sad, washed-up private detective scrounging a living from poking around in other people's business."

"You and me both," says Klaus, with a wry smile.

"Good to see you've got over the loss of your previous assistant." Gretchen turns to you. "What happened to the last one? Devoured by a firedrake, was it?"

"Fell into a bottomless pit," says Klaus. "But I'm not here to talk about that. I wanted to ask about the Time Sponge."

"Ah. A confession. Good, good." Gretchen grabs a recording device, clicks a button and thrusts it under Klaus's nose. "Why did you take it?"

You study Klaus for a reaction to this accusation. His eyes give nothing away but his lips curl into a broad grin.

"Me?" he says. "I wasn't the one who was at the scene of the crime."

"Really? Then how do you explain this?"

She holds up a grainy photograph taken at night.

You recognize the front door of the museum. Standing in front of the building is a large ghostly figure covered in white hair holding a torch. You can't be certain, but it does look rather like your boss.

"Don't give me your flimsy evidence," says Klaus. "I've lived in this town a long time. I've visited the museum before. That picture could have been taken months ago."

"It was taken last night at 2:36 a.m."

"So two and half hours after the theft," says Klaus.

"You admit it's you in the photo, then?" says Gretchen.

"I think you've got mixed up. I'm here to interrogate *you*," says Klaus. "After all, you were there *before* it was stolen, and I can think of a whole bunch of reasons why a reporter such as you would want to get hold of the sponge."

"Such as?" says Gretchen.

"It would certainly make meeting deadlines easier and give you time to find the full story."

"Oh, I always meet my deadlines." Gretchen pauses the recording device. "If there's something I don't know, I just make it up. And since I got that magic printing press, I can bring out new editions whenever I want."

"And where are you with this story?" asks Klaus.

"I haven't decided yet. Chief Inspector Darka isn't being very helpful but when is he ever?"

She presses a couple of buttons on the device and you hear Darka's voice say, "Leave me alone, you interfering banshee."

"It could have been that snake-haired Curator Doddwhistle," says Gretchen. "She could use it to pause time and stop Night Mayor Franklefink turning her museum into something this town actually needs."

She presses a button and an elderly female voice says, "Please get out of my office."

"Or perhaps it's that iddy-biddy has-been, Professor O'Leary, trying to slow down the inevitable decline of his writing career."

This time she plays a squeaky Irish voice saying, "Me? Take the Time Sponge? Utterly preposterous."

"And then there's the item's donor, Bernard the time-bending lobster," says Gretchen. "I haven't been able to find out much about him at all."

"Do you think he's involved?" asks Klaus.

"I haven't worked that out yet," says Gretchen. "But I'll find an angle. My readers love a bit of time travel. And we're hoping we can get a sponsorship with the local seafood restaurant. Now, if you don't mind, I have an article to write. Come back when you have something more interesting to say … or, maybe confess?"

"I've got my eye on you," says Klaus.

"And I have mine on you." Gretchen stands up. She laughs and the sound makes you feel dizzy and confused. Her eyes glow. She clenches her fists. A chilling wind rushes through the office, sending piles of paper cascading to the floor.

"I think we should get out of here," says Klaus.

You couldn't agree more. You move quickly down the stairs, then keep going until you can no longer hear the laughing banshee or the singing sirens.

"She gives me a headache," says Klaus. "And you don't want to believe everything she tells you."

You know he's right but you're also thinking about the photograph of him outside the museum. Could he be keeping something from you?

"We should find out more about this lobster," says Klaus. "Haventry's Other Library is the best place for that but you need to be connected to the university to get in. I'll call Professor O'Leary and ask him to show us around ... unless—" He pauses and looks at you. You wonder if he can see the suspicion in your eyes.

"Are you OK? You look like you have something on your mind."

You reply:

? "No, it's nothing. Let's go to the library."

Turn to page 81
HAVENTRY'S OTHER LIBRARY

? "Klaus, you need to tell me what's going on. I know you haven't told me everything."

Turn to page 77
ACCUSING KLAUS

ACCUSING KLAUS

TELLING YOUR BOSS THAT YOU think he hasn't been entirely honest with you is an unsettling experience, but you hold your nerve. You tell him you suspect he's withholding information. You list everything on your mind that has led to this conclusion. You stop short of suggesting that you're beginning to wonder if he might have something to do with the theft.

After you've said your piece, there's an uncomfortable silence.

Klaus sighs.

"You're a good assistant and I shouldn't have lied to you," he says, "but you're right that I didn't tell you everything at the start. I'll tell you now, though, because I need your mind on the case and I can't have you getting distracted by any thought that I might be involved in this."

You're sitting in the car, stroking Watson's furry seats. From the happy panting, you can tell the car is enjoying the attention, but your focus is on your yeti boss. He pops open the glove compartment and pulls out a mobile phone. He taps something in and then you hear his voicemail on speakerphone.

"You have no new messages. You have one saved message. To play the saved message pres—" Klaus presses a number, and the phone beeps.

You don't recognize the echoey voice that speaks.

"Klaus Solstaag," it says, "you don't know me but I know you. I need your help. I am Bernard the time-bending lobster. I am calling from the distant future … a time known only as … the Tuesday after next. Someone has stolen an object that belongs to me. The Time Sponge has been taken from the Museum of Magical Objects and Precious Stones. Or it will be. Or it will have been by the time I have finished this message. It's hard to say. From where I'm calling, everything is the past."

You're doing your best to follow what the voice is saying.

"Even if it hasn't happened yet, you will not be able to prevent it. The theft is already drawn in the tides of time, but you must recover my precious sponge. You see, I am not just the owner of the sponge. I am its protector. For if it fell into the wrong hands, time could be frozen forever. I have seen the future and I already know you will take this case. And yet it will be your assistant – not you – who claims this prize. You need help with this one. You cannot do this alone. This is Bernard the time-bending lobster saying goodbye for now … and for then and for not quite yet. Goodbye."

Klaus looks embarrassed. "I suppose I thought I could prove him wrong. I mean, you're a good assistant but I thought I should be able to do this on my own. But I've been investigating this since 2 a.m. and still don't have the answer. So now you know. I…" He places a hand on your shoulder. "I need you."

He smiles at you apologetically and you know he's finally told you the whole truth.

"Now, I think it's high time we found out a bit more about this time-bending lobster who hired me. We should find some answers at the library." He looks at his watch. "I'll call Professor O'Leary and have him meet us outside."

He turns the key and Watson lets out a barking rev of his engine. Other options are whirling around inside your head but you agree that right now, you should get to the library and find out whatever you can about this mysterious lobster.

"That's right, boy," says Klaus, patting the dashboard. "You'll be able to say hello to Drouble." He turns back to you. "And from now on, I promise I'll tell you everything."

? Turn to page 81
HAVENTRY'S OTHER LIBRARY

HAVENTRY'S OTHER LIBRARY

Most people in Haventry use the internet when they want to find something out, but, since you took this job on the Shady Side of town, you've discovered that some answers can't be found online.

Sure, the internet has plenty of pictures and descriptions of goblins, ghosts, monsters and various types of undead creatures that roam these streets, but precious little of it matches reality. When seeking the truth about more extraordinary things, it pays to visit Haventry's *Other* Library. Unlike the modern, large-windowed building in the centre of town, Haventry's *Other* Library is easy to miss. It's on the same side of town as the university, and it's sandwiched between a café run by werewolves called Big Bites and a coffee shop run by vampires called Coffee & Coffins.

You and your boss are standing outside with Professor O'Leary. It's raining and the leprechaun is looking up at the sky.

"Hoping for a rainbow?" asks Klaus.

"Is that a leprechaun joke? Because I don't appreciate it," replies the professor, clutching his briefcase. "Remember, this is a reference library. You are forbidden from removing books."

"You think I don't know that?" says Klaus.

"I was addressing your human friend," replies the professor, raising his eyebrows at you. "You know that, strictly speaking, they're not really allowed in here."

"Don't worry about my assistant," says Klaus.

"Yes, well. We do have these rules for a reason," says Professor O'Leary. "But since it's you, Klaus, I suppose it's all right."

As you enter the reception area, a low growl alerts you to a pair of Dobermans behind the desk. One rests its head on the counter. The other appears to be reading a book.

"Top of the morning to you, Drouble," says

Professor O'Leary.

Both heads turn to look at you and you realize that they share a body.

"Watson is outside," says Klaus.

The dog turns its heads to look at Klaus's car, parked outside. Both mouths bark. Watson responds with a beep of his horn and an excited little wheel spin.

"Drouble used to love running around Snark Park with Watson," explains Klaus. "Not that I can take Watson there any more because his tyres rip up the grass and he's still rusty from the time he chased a duck into the lake."

You're a little unnerved by the way one of the heads is looking at you, with its large jaws gaping and a long droplet of spittle hanging from its yellow teeth.

"He can smell that you're human," says Professor O'Leary.

"Don't worry," says Klaus. "Drouble is a big softy."

"Unless you try to remove a book, in which case he'll tear you limb from limb, so he will," adds the professor.

You're relieved to see the sturdy leads attached to collars around both of the dog's necks and chained to the back wall.

The main library has high ceilings and tall shelves lined with weighty tomes that block out the light trying to shine through the grimy windows. You, Klaus and Professor O'Leary are the only people inside.

"They have a good collection of all of my literary efforts here of course," says Professor O'Leary with a fake modest laugh.

"You mean both books?" clarifies Klaus.

"Yes, *A History of the Future* was such a big hit that the publishers were taken by surprise when my sequel, *The Future of the Past,* sold even more copies."

"You must be due another one soon," says Klaus.

"You can't hurry these things," replies Professor O'Leary, scurrying down the corridor. "I've made a start, though."

He opens his briefcase and pulls out a few sheets of paper. He clearly hasn't got very far.

"Hm. I won't hold my breath, then," says Klaus.

"Anyway, you'll want to take a look at Bernard's autobiography," says the professor, changing the subject. "If memory serves, it's along here."

The area is labelled *UNLIKELY LIFE STORIES*. Professor O'Leary scans the bottom two shelves but is unable to locate the book. He finds a ladder and climbs up. As he gets higher, occasionally his foot sends a book tumbling down. Klaus bats them away.

"A-ha," cries Professor O'Leary. "This is the one. Get ready to catch."

UNLIKELY LIFE STORIES

You hold out your hands as Professor O'Leary drops the book. It lands heavily in your arms and falls open. Both pages are blank. Klaus leans over to take a closer look.

You flick to another page. Then another.

"There's nothing written in it," says Klaus.

Professor O'Leary climbs back down and takes a look. "Oh, I was afraid that might be the case. You see, as the author is able to bend time, the words only exist on the page when he's in our current time zone."

"What does that mean?" says Klaus patiently.

"Time travel is always confusing," says Professor O'Leary. "But put simply, if Bernard's visiting the past, you can't read the book because it deals with a present he hasn't yet lived. If he's in the future then you can't read it because he hasn't written it yet."

"Er…" Klaus scratches his head. You're feeling similarly confused.

"As I like to say," says Professor O'Leary, "when it comes to time travel, sometimes it's best to just accept what you've been told."

"So the words will appear when he's back in the present?" says Klaus.

"Precisely," says the leprechaun.

"Any idea when that's likely to be?"

"None whatsoever," Professor O'Leary replies cheerily.

"Why does he keep jumping around in time anyway?" asks Klaus. "It seems like suspicious behaviour if you ask me."

"There's nothing suspicious about it," says Professor O'Leary. "Time-bending lobsters such as Bernard have a different perception of time. While we follow time's arrow in one direction, they surf on the tides of time. They are explorers, protectors and preservers of the space-time continuum. They're also very mysterious. It's their thing."

Klaus glances at you. You shrug. You haven't a clue what Professor O'Leary is talking about but he does seem to know more about this missing sponge – and its mysterious owner – than anyone else you've spoken to.

"It's a shame, to be sure, but you'll have to put the book back on the shelf. Sorry to have wasted your time."

Klaus steps between you and the professor, looks you in the eye and says, "You heard what he said and you know what to do."

He begins walking away with the professor, but

something in his voice when he just spoke gives you pause to reflect. You still have the book in your hand. Does he want you to take it? Or should you do as the professor told you and return it? You certainly don't like the idea of Drouble finding you with a stolen book, but it seems like your boss was trying to tell you something. Time is running out. Professor O'Leary could turn around and spot you at any moment.

You have to decide.

? Do you quickly slip the book into your bag?

Turn to page 89

THE BOOK THIEF

? Or put the book back on the shelf?

Turn to page 92

WHERE IS THE BOOK?

THE BOOK THIEF

YOU DROP THE BOOK INTO your bag and hurry after Klaus and Professor O'Leary. Your shoes squeak noisily on the polished floor. You aren't feeling too anxious until you step into the foyer to find that both of Drouble's heads are staring at you.

You try to stroll as casually as possible, but one head is sniffing while the other growls. Are they trained to pick up the scent of every library book? Can they see through your bag? Or maybe they can see into your mind and the scrambled thoughts that lie within.

Did you interpret Klaus's actions correctly? Did he really want you to take the book? He has been here before. Surely he knows if there's any real danger of detection.

The dog's right head is snarling. The left one barks.

"Quiet down, Drouble," says Professor O'Leary. "No one's taken anything."

"He's just excited to see Watson," says Klaus.

You glance out of the window and see Watson bouncing up and down enthusiastically. Drouble barks at the car. You feel a massive sense of relief as you exit the building.

"Best of luck with the case," says Professor O'Leary. "The Time Sponge is a remarkable object. When you squeeze it, even the raindrops hang in the air like jewels. I hope you find the thief."

"Thanks. I hope it doesn't turn out to be you," says Klaus.

Professor O'Leary lets out a short nervous laugh. "Honestly, Klaus, I'm a well-respected author. My new book is coming along nicely."

"So I see," says Klaus.

The professor holds up his bag and waves it around. Is it your imagination that it looks heavier than before? You wonder if Professor O'Leary also took something from the library.

"I'm doing an author signing at Stonewater Books later," he says. "Gretchen Barfly-Sewer's going to be interviewing me about my work. Maybe I'll see you there."

He hurries away and you get into the car. Watson is overexcited about seeing Drouble but Klaus calms him down with the threat of a trip to the mechanics. As Klaus pulls away, you take the book out and slip it into the glove compartment.

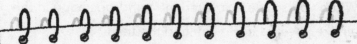

You're not sure if your boss spots you doing this. His eyes are on the road and his thoughts are on the case.

"Right," he says. "I think it's time to do some background checks on everyone."

? Turn to page 95
HOT CHOCOLATE, COLD TRUTHS

WHERE IS THE BOOK?

YOU'RE STANDING OUTSIDE THE LIBRARY, wondering if you made the right decision. If that book is the only way of finding out whether Bernard the time-bending lobster is nearby, then maybe you should have taken it, but it's too late to change your mind now.

"Best of luck with the case," says Professor O'Leary. "The Time Sponge is a remarkable object. When you squeeze it, even the raindrops hang in the air like jewels. I hope you find the thief."

"Thanks. I hope it doesn't turn out to be you," replies Klaus.

Professor O'Leary lets out a nervous laugh.

"Honestly, Klaus, I'm a well-respected author." He pulls out a handful of paper from his bag. You're not sure but it seems thicker than the last time you saw it. "In fact, I'm doing an author signing at Stonewater Books later. Gretchen Barfly-Sewer's going to be interviewing me about my new book."

"If you ever get round to finishing it," says Klaus.

"You can't rush genius," replies the professor. "Don't worry, it will be finished in no time. Maybe I'll see you there."

He rushes off and you get into the car. You can tell that Watson is excited to see Drouble because he is panting and bouncing up and down, making an awful creaking noise.

"Take it easy," says Klaus. "It's not good for your suspension. You don't want the mechanic to have to take another look under your bonnet, do you?"

Instantly, Watson calms down.

"Good lad." Klaus turns to you. "He's not a fan of going to mechanics. So? Where's the book?"

He can tell what you are going to say before you speak.

"You haven't got it? Why do you think I blocked the professor's view?" he asks. "Please don't tell me you were worried about Drouble. That two-headed dog is a big pussycat. Oh well, we'll just have to find another way of keeping tabs on this lobster. The question still remains, which one of our suspects is looking most likely?"

You wonder this too. Pieces are falling into place but before you begin the hard work of trying to decipher all of these different meanings, it is time to do some background checks on your suspects.

? Turn to page 95
HOT CHOCOLATE, COLD TRUTHS

HOT CHOCOLATE, COLD TRUTHS

THERE'S A POINT DURING ANY investigation when you need to return to your office and take stock of where you've got to. As soon as you step inside the door, Klaus drops to his knees and starts rummaging through boxes of newspaper cuttings, maps, photographs and notes from previous cases.

He sends you out to buy a couple of hot chocolates from a stall on the corner run by hobgoblins. You're grateful to have something to warm your hands on. Klaus likes to keep the office cool. It helps him think. When you return, the fans are on full blast.

You're wearing two jumpers, a pair of gloves and a coat but you're still cold. You clasp your hot chocolate and try to stop your teeth from chattering. The place is even messier now and Klaus has clearly been busy researching.

"Why can I never find a pen that works?" he moans. He scribbles on a piece of paper, then lobs the useless pen over his shoulder. You reluctantly hand him yours, hoping he'll manage not to break this one.

"Thanks," he says. "While you've been out, I've been going through our possible suspects. Let's lay down the facts and see where we're at."

He tries to write something down, but pushes so hard that the nib goes straight through the paper. He shrugs, yanks the paper away and continues writing on the desk instead.

He writes *THE MERMAIDS* then draws a circle around the words.

"The three mermaids, all employees of Mermail, delivered the sponge to the museum in the first place. When we arrived, Rigmarole was looking at the tyre marks on the ramp. Mermaids travel everywhere by wheelchairs when they're out of the water so maybe they had to make a quick getaway."

It makes sense that mermaids would use wheelchairs to get around the city. Even the people of Haventry might notice something odd about three fish-tailed postal workers flapping down the road.

"They would have known where the sponge was being kept, and the security involved. They had the means but did they have the motive? Plus, why would you deliver something and then steal it?" Klaus leaves the question hanging for a moment then says, "Well, I have a theory about that. I found this in the *Haventry Chronicle*."

Even though the *Chronicle* is read by Haventry's more normal townsfolk, it does sometimes include stories that provide clues. He drops the newspaper in front of you. It's dated today.

Police are asking people to look out for three thieves in wheelchairs, suspected of stealing from a number of shops.

"There seems to be nothing these three won't take," said one newsagent. "And when I challenged them, it was like they didn't even know they were stealing."

"Three thieves in wheelchairs?" says Klaus. "A coincidence? I don't think so. I'm told mermaids don't carry human money – they only have cockles and shells. Maybe they've got a problem stealing things or maybe there's another reason. Whatever it is, we still can't rule them out."

He gives you a moment to allow this to sink in before moving on to the next suspect. He starts to write CURATOR DODDWHISTLE, but the pen snaps halfway through. He grabs another but it doesn't work. Thinking he's dipping it in an inkwell, he plunges the pen into his hot chocolate. He doesn't notice his mistake and writes the rest of the name in brown milky liquid.

"Doddwhistle's run that museum for years but Night Mayor Franklefink wants to turn it into a shopping centre," he says. "He's not been afraid to make enemies since he won the election."

He waves a leaflet in front of you. It says VOTE FRANKLEFINK on the front and has a picture of a white-haired man in a lab coat. You recognize him as Dr Franklefink, the monster-making scientist who was recently elected Night Mayor of Haventry. Klaus opens the leaflet and points to a paragraph at the bottom of the second page. You read:

MAKE THE MUSEUM
HISTORY!

As part of my pledge to modernize this town, I will shut down Haventry's tired old Museum of Magical Objects and Precious Stones and replace it with a brand new mall where members of the Shady Side community can find all the shops catering for their needs under one roof.

"Doddwhistle can't have been happy when Franklefink became Night Mayor," Klaus continues. "He plans to shut her down. Maybe she's hoping to use the Time Sponge to halt time and save her museum. But it's true the place isn't as popular as it used to be."

You're still reading the leaflet. On the other side is a picture of Franklefink shaking hands with Chief Inspector Darka, and the words: *I promise to be tough on crime.*

Klaus sees it too. "I suppose if Night Mayor Franklefink wants to shut down the museum, he might have paid someone to remove the sponge in an attempt to sabotage the exhibition, but as he's not in town I'm not putting his name on our list. However, one person who definitely did have the opportunity, is our leprechaun time-travel expert, Professor O'Leary."

Klaus grabs a newspaper and tears out the name from a headline that reads:

O'LEARY, OH DEARY!

He slams the torn-out name on the desk.

"It seems our leprechaun may have been forced to give up a crock of gold," says Klaus. "I found this in a recent *News of the Unusual*." He hands the rest of the cutting to you. It reads:

Popular science writer Professor Timothy O'Leary was red-faced with embarrassment when it was revealed today that he has to hand back the money he was paid by his publisher after his failure to finish a third book to follow his previous successes, *A History of the Future* and *The Future of the Past*.

"Everyone's been waiting for that third book for years now," says Klaus. "This makes it sound like his publishers have given up on him. If it's about money, then the Time Sponge would surely fetch a fair bit."

You've found another pen in your drawer and you hurriedly jot down your notes on Klaus's reasoning. It's at times like these, when the temperature is low and his thoughts are free-flowing, that he so often hits on the thing that will lead you to the solution. It's your job to listen and make some sense of it all.

"But of course, that article was written by our next suspect." Klaus looks for somewhere to write the person's name. You edge away, not wanting him to take (and break) another of your pens. The whole office is a mess and the wastepaper basket is overflowing. Klaus picks it up, turns it upside down, tipping out its contents, then writes on the bottom of the bin: *GRETCHEN BARFLY-SEWER.*

"It's hard to find out much about Gretchen because she writes all the news – and half of it's made up! She twists everything. Her magic printing press can bring out countless editions throughout the day and she decides what her readers should think, then she makes sure they think it. That also means we can't trust anything she might tell us."

Going by what you've learned about this banshee

reporter, you agree with him.

"This whole business is very popular with her readers, though. Could she have stolen the sponge just to generate the very story she's reporting on? It's a stretch but it's not impossible. She was certainly one of the last people to see it before it was stolen, as we know she was at the press night. But she left the room at 10 p.m. when Darka locked the door and settled in to guard it, while Rigmarole went outside."

Klaus grabs another copy of the *News Of the Unusual* and tears out the names of the final two suspects:

DS RIGMAROLE

CHIEF INSPECTOR DARKA

"Our bullish chief was personally guarding the sponge, and remember, the simplest solution to a locked-door mystery is that it was the person with the key. But why? If you could freeze time, you could catch a fair few criminals but would Darka commit a crime to stop a crime? Maybe. Or perhaps he's keeping me away from this case because he knows he's messed up and he's trying to hide his tracks. We know he drank a fair bit of sparkling pop last night. And remember, Rigmarole was nearby too. I'm not sure she has the guts to carry off something like this but I've included her name so she doesn't feel left out."

Klaus may be quick to dismiss the elf officer, but you have your suspicions about her. She struck you as ambitious and you didn't like the way she spoke to you and your boss as though she knew better than you. You might be new to detective work but you've still got some idea what you're doing.

You look at your list of suspects. One of them took the sponge. You don't know which one, but you feel as though you understand why. Since you heard about it, you've wondered more than once what it must feel like to hold the sponge. You'd be surprised if the same thought hasn't occurred to your boss. You want to solve the case but you also want to find the sponge so you can squeeze it and feel its power.

"So?" says Klaus.

You look up at him, jolted out of your thoughts.

"What do you think?" he asks. "We know that two

of our suspects will be in the same place. Gretchen is interviewing Professor O'Leary at Stonewater Books. We could see if the mermaids really are shoplifting by going into town. Or we could return to the museum and see what we can find out there. Or maybe we should head to the station and ask the police to help us with our enquiries. It's up to you."

? Go to see Professor O'Leary and Gretchen Barfly-Sewer at the book reading.

Turn to page 105

BOOKSHOP BANTER

? Go to look for the mermaids at the shops.

Turn to page 112

SOMETHING FISHY

? Return to the museum.

Turn to page 120

WITCH FINDERS

? Got to the police station.

Turn to page 127

HANDCUFFS AND ACCUSATIONS

BOOKSHOP BANTER

THE TRAFFIC IS ALWAYS BAD in this part of town. Right now, Watson is quietly growling at a set of temporary lights. Klaus taps his steering wheel impatiently. The air conditioning is on full blast, blowing his hair back from his face. He switches on the radio.

You hear Nick Grimm say, "Breaking news coming in. Chief Inspector Darka has just made an official statement regarding the theft of the Time Sponge, in which he said the UPF would be releasing the name of the prime suspect very shortly. More on that story as we get information but, right now, here's another monster hit from—"

Klaus switches it off.

"So Darka has a name," he mumbles. "I wonder which tree he's barking up. Talking of which, what's wrong with you, Watson? You're supposed to be parking not barking!"

Klaus is trying to park outside Stonewater Books but Watson is growling at a white van parked a little further down the road. This kind of thing is not unusual. It's one of the many problems with driving a car that used to be a dog.

"I tell you what," says Klaus. "You go in and save us a couple of seats while I find somewhere he's willing to park."

You get out and close the door behind you. Watson drives away and you notice three figures dressed in dark blue. They are all in wheelchairs, heading into a department store on the other side of the road. When you look more closely, you notice large bulges where their legs should be.

It's the mermaids. For a moment, you consider following them, but you've come here to see the leprechaun and the banshee. Klaus is counting on you to stick to the plan.

When you enter, Professor O'Leary's talk is already underway. You thought it might be difficult to find a seat but there are plenty available. Gretchen Barfly-Sewer sits next to the professor, glancing at her watch as he talks. You find an empty row and sit down. The audience is so small that it's not hard to spot the witches, Bridget and Burnella Milkbird.

Both have their hands raised. Their enormous monster Bootsy sits in between them, emitting a low rumbling moan of "Booooooooooks".

"Let's have a question from the audience," says Gretchen. "Bridget Milkbird."

"Thank you. Yes, I have a very important question," says Bridget. "So what exactly is a crock of gold and how do you find the end of the rainbow?"

Professor O'Leary doesn't look impressed by the question. "Ha, well, you see that's a common misconception about leprechauns—"

The witches aren't interested in his answer. They are both cackling with laughter.

"I only came here to get my shoes fixed," says Burnella.

"I think that's elves," says Bridget.

Burnella turns around and spies you. "Oh, look, the amateur sleuth is here. Hello."

She waves at you. You raise your hand and smile but these witches have always unnerved you. You happen to know that it was a witch who turned poor Watson into a car in the first place. He seems happy enough with his lot, but you'd rather not be turned into anything.

"Where's your boss?"

You're about to answer when you hear the door open and Klaus enters. He sits next to you. "What have I missed?"

"Excuse me," says Professor O'Leary irritably. "I'm supposed to be the focus here. Are there any questions about my new book?"

"Sorry," says Klaus in a loud whisper.

"I have one," says Gretchen. "When exactly are we going to be able to read it? I heard that you had to hand back the money you were paid to write it."

"You can't rush these things, but as you can see, I'm making good progress." He taps a pile of paper on the desk. "Slowly but surely."

"You can't sit around and wait for inspiration if you're a journalist," says Gretchen. "I have deadlines. I have readers hanging on my every word. This morning

I wrote three thousand words before breakfast."

"Yes, but my words bear some relation to the truth," says Professor O'Leary. "Anyone can make up a story if they don't have to worry about facts."

"I make the facts," snaps Gretchen.

"I have a question for Professor O'Leary," says Klaus, raising his hand.

Gretchen turns to him. "Ah, Klaus Solstaag. Go ahead."

"It's about the Time Sponge," says Klaus.

The witches turn to look at him.

"The Time Sponge is a fascinating object and one about which I know a lot, so I am happy to talk about its remarkable power," says Professor O'Leary. "What is your question?"

"I just wondered if the sponge could be used by a journalist to freeze time and write three thousand words before breakfast?"

Now everyone in the shop is staring at your boss.

"Ah, well, um…" Professor O'Leary is clearly rattled, but Gretchen is laughing.

"What an interesting question," she says. "Especially since my sources at the UPF station suggest that the most likely suspect is a disgraced former UPF officer who now works as a private investigator. Oh, and he's a yeti."

"You're suggesting I had something to do with this?" says Klaus, his nostrils flaring. "I find things. I don't take them."

"We're good at finding things too," says Bridget. "Maybe we could help you."

"I don't think he could afford us," says Burnella.

"I'm sorry," says Professor O'Leary. "We are here to discuss my work. Does anyone have any questions about time?"

"Yes, what time does this finish?" asks Bridget.

Burnella cackles with laughter. "Never mind pausing time, I feel like this has been dragging on forever," she says.

"Foreverrrrr," repeats Bootsy.

"Quiet down, Bootsy," say both witches.

Professor O'Leary is on his feet, although this actually makes him shorter than when he was sitting down. "I have never been so insulted in my life," he says angrily and storms off.

Klaus gets up too. You follow him out of the bookshop and into the street. Klaus pulls his hat over his head, hiding his yeti features from anyone who happens to be passing.

"I'm not ready to rule out either Gretchen or O'Leary," says Klaus. "This plot is thickening faster than gravy on a gas hob. Having heard what Gretchen's source said about the police suspecting me, though, I think we'd better get down to the station."

? Do you agree with Klaus?

Turn to page 127
HANDCUFFS AND ACCUSATIONS

? Or should you tell him about having spotted the mermaids?

Turn to page 112
SOMETHING FISHY

SOMETHING FISHY

HAVENTRY DOESN'T HAVE A SHOPPING area dedicated to the Shady Side community. Instead, its more unusual residents have to blend in among the everyday townsfolk in their shopping centres and high streets.

Mud Market Retail Park is a dreary little collection of shops just off the high street. A light drizzle hangs in the air as the shoppers trudge from store to store. Your eyes take in every detail. You recognize the clown handing balloon animals to children as an ex-zombie you know by the name of Deadzo. What appears to be a woman pushing a pram is actually two goblins stacked on top of each other pushing what you suspect may be a baby dragon, judging by the amount of smoke pouring out.

You nudge Klaus when you spot the mermaids entering a clothes shop. They're all in wheelchairs with blankets thrown over their tails.

"Stay close," says Klaus. "We don't want to attract any attention."

You can't help smiling. Klaus is so tall he has to duck to get inside. It amazes you how he doesn't draw more astonished gazes, but somehow he manages to blend in. Which is more than can be said for the mermaids. As soon as you enter the shop, you can hear throaty laughter and loud tail-slapping. You find them in the swimwear section.

The one with green hair is holding up a bikini. "What do you think, Annabelle?"

"It's too skimpy, Amelie," replies the purple-haired mermaid. "Wouldn't you say, Fred?"

"Yep," says the only male mermaid. "I've had dental floss with more material on it."

"And look at these, Fred." Annabelle holds a large pair of swimming trunks up and places them on her head.

"Hey, I know a song about that," he says, clearing his throat then singing at the top of his voice.

"Excuse me, sir. Can I help you with anything?" says a nervous-looking shop assistant.

"No, just browsing," replies Fred.

"I see. Well, please could you refrain from singing? It disturbs the other customers." The assistant walks away but you can tell she's keeping her eye on these strange characters.

"Hi there," says Klaus as he approaches them. The mermaids spin their wheelchairs around to face him.

"Yes? Do you work here? We're looking for the waterproofs," says Amelie.

"Have we met before?" Annabelle scrutinizes you both.

"Sorry about her," says Fred. "She has a condition."

"We all have a condition," adds Amelie cheerily.

"Show them the card," says Fred.

"Oh yes, the card," says Annabelle.

She reaches under her blanket and pulls out a card that reads:

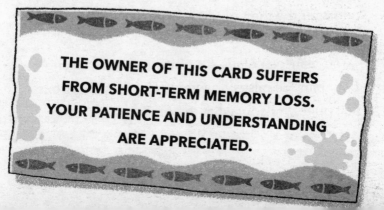

THE OWNER OF THIS CARD SUFFERS FROM SHORT-TERM MEMORY LOSS. YOUR PATIENCE AND UNDERSTANDING ARE APPRECIATED.

Klaus gives it a cursory glance. "Yes, so you were telling me about the disappearance of the Time Sponge." Klaus winks at you. He's using their forgetfulness to his advantage.

"Were we?" says Amelie. "I thought we were talking to the other one about that…"

"Which one?" asks Annabelle.

"You know … big … bully."

"A big bully?" asks Klaus.

"Bully, not a bully," says Annabelle. "You know, half-bull."

"Ah. So what did Chief Inspector Darka have to say?" asks Klaus.

"He thought it was taken by someone called… No, it's gone," says Amelie.

"Karl? Carlos? Something like that," says Annabelle.

Amelie nods. "Whatever the name was, he said he had it on good authority that this … whatever his name is … was spotted at the scene of the crime soon after the theft of … whatever it was that was stolen."

You glance at Klaus. It's obvious they're talking about him. He raises his eyebrows at you, but you can't quite work out what this look means. You've never had a case in which your boss was a suspect. It's unnerving.

"The name you're reaching for is Klaus," he says to the mermaids.

"Klaus, yes, that's it," says Amelie.

"What's what?" asks Annabelle.

"I'm not sure," admits Amelie.

"I think he's saying that he's the thief," says Fred.

"I am not," states Klaus. "But I would be interested to know what else you keep on your laps. As would the store security, I'm guessing."

Since you've been talking to them, all three have picked up various items of swimwear and absent-mindedly put them under their blankets.

"Outrageous!" says Annabelle. "It's more likely to be in your pocket than under our blankets."

"What is?" asks Fred.

"The Lime Sponge?" suggests Amelie.

"Time Sponge," says Klaus irritably. "Why would I be looking for it if it was me who took it?" You wonder if Klaus sounds a bit defensive.

"He can't even remember if he took it," says Amelie.

"He's worse than us," adds Annabelle.

"Who is?" asks Fred.

"This is getting us nowhere," says Klaus. "Come on, let's get out of here."

You turn and walk out of the shop, but the mermaids follow, laughing and slapping their tails loudly under the blankets. As they reach the door, the alarm sounds and a security guard soon appears, wearing a hi-vis jacket.

"What do you want?" says Amelie.

"Please can I see what you have under there?" asks the guard.

"You certainly cannot." But as she says this, a pair of swimming goggles fall to the floor. "Oh, how did that get there?"

"I think we'd better have a word in my office," says the security guard.

"It was an accident, officer. We have a condition. Who's got the card?" Annabelle protests. But the guard is already ushering them off. You wonder how they will prevent him noticing the large fishtails hidden under their blankets.

Klaus turns to you. "I don't know about you but I'm ready to strike these mermaids off my suspect list. Forgetful shoplifters, they may be. Criminal masterminds, they definitely are not."

You nod in agreement, but your mind is

elsewhere. As far as the police are concerned, your boss is a prime suspect. You feel conflicted. You want to defend him, but you also want to learn the truth. Klaus always tells you that everyone lies. And in this case, that includes him. Has he told you the whole truth?

"Are you all right?" asks Klaus.

You shake yourself. What are you doing, doubting your own boss? You can't seriously suspect Klaus. You tell him you're fine.

"I think we need to speak to Darka," says Klaus. "But where is he most likely to be?"

? Should you try the museum?

Turn to page 120
WITCH FINDERS

? Or is it time to visit the police station?

Turn to page 127
HANDCUFFS AND ACCUSATIONS

WITCH FINDERS

THERE ARE NO POLICE OFFICERS guarding the front of the museum this time. A sign on the door reads: *TEMPORARILY CLOSED* and police tape blocks access to the front entrance.

"Let's use the back door," Klaus says.

You follow him around the side of the building, where two ugly gargoyles jut from the corners. One of them spots you coming.

"Hey, Spitz," says the one on the left. "Look who's back."

"Who is it, Granite?" The hideous carving on the right attempts to angle his body around but can't quite move enough to see.

"It's Klaus Solstaag," says Granite. "Darka warned us you might come poking around here again."

"You're not allowed in," says Spitz, who is only able to see you out of the corner of his eye.

"Are you two working for the UPF now?" says Klaus.

"Technically, we're council property and we're—" Spitz is interrupted by a pigeon landing on his head. "Hey! Get off me!"

"Stop bothering Captain Flaps," says Granite. "He's only being friendly, aren't you?" The pigeon flaps its wings and flies from Spitz to Granite. "See. He's my friend."

"Friends don't go to the toilet on your head," says Spitz.

"Some do," replies Granite.

"Let's leave them to it," whispers Klaus, aware that no matter what they say, the gargoyles are unable to prevent you entering.

He pushes the door open but it slams shut, as though caught by a sudden breeze. He tries a second time but the same thing happens again.

The gargoyles laugh.

121

"Ha. Not so clever now, are you?" says Spitz.

"How are you doing that?" asks Klaus.

"We're not," says Granite. "They are."

The door swings open of its own accord and, in a puff of purple smoke, the witches, Burnella and Bridget Milkbird, appear in front of you.

"Surprise," says Bridget dryly.

Burnella lowers her head and sniffs you with her warty nose. "And everyone likes surprises," she hisses in your ear.

"What are you two doing here?" asks Klaus.

Burnella holds up a card:

Burnella and Bridget Milkbird
WITCH FINDERS
All lost things, we shall locate,
We charge a fair, flat, hourly rate,
Hubble, bubble, toil and trouble
(Except at weekends when we charge double!)

"It's a side-line," says Burnella. "The catering business is slow and we fancied a fresh challenge."

"So we set up this business. And Doddwhistle is an old friend of ours," says Bridget.

"Oh yes, we knew her when she had a full head full of virile young vipers," adds Burnella.

"And she's brought us in because she wouldn't trust that old minotaur Darka to solve a crossword clue, let alone find the Time Sponge," says Bridget.

"But … when did she employ you?" asks Klaus suspiciously.

"Why? Jealous she didn't ask you?" says Burnella. "Pretty hard to ask you when you're one of the main suspects."

"Me?" says Klaus.

"That's what we've heard." Bridget turns to you. "I hope your boss is on your list of suspects."

You take a step back and they cackle with laughter.

"Bootsy is inside now," says Burnella. "He's combing the area for clues."

You hear a massive crash from inside the museum.

"You clumsy oaf!" yells Bridget.

"Honestly, that monster," says Burnella.

They turn and swoop down the corridor. Klaus takes his opportunity and follows. You're hot on his heels and inside the exhibit room before either witch can stop you.

The Time Sponge is still missing of course, but the other exhibits are all present and correct.

The Occasional Lamp keeps disappearing and reappearing. The Memory Basin is full of murky water that will reveal flashes of the past. The Fortune Cookie Dough, however, has fallen foul of Bootsy's clumsy evidence collecting. The bowl is on the floor and its gooey contents have spilled out.

"We give you one job," says Bridget.

"Or quite a lot of jobs," says Burnella.

"Baaaad Boootsy," says the monster gloomily.

"I still haven't worked out how the thief got in and out of this locked room," says Klaus.

"There are so many possibilities," says Bridget. "They could have magicked in. Or climbed in through the window."

"Or just used a spare key if it was Doddwhistle who did it." Burnella taps her nose and winks.

"That doesn't make sense," says Klaus. "Doddwhistle hired you so why would she … er… hold on."

It's unlike Klaus to lose his train of thought but he's distracted by the spilled cookie dough.

"Look," he says. "It's spelling something out."

Sure enough, the cookie dough is bubbling and popping. It's moving of its own accord, as though controlled by some mysterious invisible force.

The gooey mixture is forming letters. It's going to reveal something that will be said in the future.

Klaus reads it out loud as it appears. "The answer is at the police station."

"Ooh, that's clever," says Bridget.

"Cleeeeveeeeer," moans Bootsy.

"Button it, mop head," says Burnella.

"This dough records phrases that will be spoken or written in the future but, since you just said it, for all we know it was predicting the moment you would read it out loud," says Bridget.

"What?" asks Burnella.

"I'm not sure," admits her sister.

"Whatever it means," says Klaus. "I think we'd better get to the station."

"Yes, good idea," says Bridget. "You run along and do that."

Both witches move their arms like swaying tree branches and mutter incantations under their breath. A strange yellow smoke drifts up from the floorboards and envelops you. You feel a surge of panic. This is witch magic. You open your mouth to scream in fear, but you blink and find yourself standing on the pavement outside the police station.

"Well, I guess we'd better head inside, then," says Klaus.

You have your reservations about heading into the station but your doubts are outweighed by your eagerness to learn what's going on.

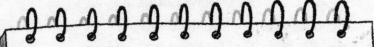

? You enter UPF the station.

Turn to page 127
HANDCUFFS AND ACCUSATIONS

HANDCUFFS AND ACCUSATIONS

STEPPING INTO THE **UPF** STATION is an unnerving experience. There are rows of desks where all kinds of cops are interviewing a range of dubious-looking characters. These representatives of the Shady Side's murky underbelly are some of the slimiest, grimiest, hairiest and scariest creatures you've ever laid eyes on.

You keep your head down, avoiding eye contact. Klaus is standing at the counter, impatiently asking the bespectacled centaur desk sergeant why he's having to wait so long.

"Chief Inspector Darka will be with you presently," says the centaur, waving a fly away with his tail. "Please take a seat."

You both sit down on plastic chairs just as a tall, pale-faced figure strides through the precinct, her scarlet hair billowing behind her.

"Ah, Klaus. You decided to hand yourself in after all, did you? Good, good."

"Gretchen," says Klaus. "What brings you here?"

"I've popped in for my daily update on UPF activities," replies the terrifying banshee reporter.

"Yes, you can go through to the waiting room," says the desk sergeant, swatting another fly. "Our press officer will be with you shortly."

"Very well," says Gretchen. "I look forward to hearing all about what you've been up to, Klaus."

She leaves, and you're unsure if the cold draft comes from the door or from the banshee herself, but you're relieved she's gone. Klaus turns back to the desk sergeant.

"Listen," he says. "I'm not your average Joe here. I used to be a Detective Inspector."

A door swings open and Chief Inspector Darka steps through. You spot a pair of cuffs in his gloved hand.

"Until you gave up on us," he says.

"Darka," says Klaus, puffing out his chest. "I'm here about the Time Sponge—"

"Klaus Solstaag." There's no hint of a smile on the minotaur's face. "I'm glad you decided to come in voluntarily. It makes the job easier."

"What's that supposed to mean?" asks Klaus.

Darka jangles the handcuffs. "Please don't make this harder than it needs to be."

"Harder?" Klaus glances at you. It's rare for him to worry but that's precisely the look you see in his eyes.

"What are you talking about? I'm here to ask you about the Time Sponge."

"A case that I told you to stay away from but in which, I fear, you are more involved than you've been letting on," counters Chief Inspector Darka.

"Can we speak in private?" asks Klaus, aware that every pair of eyes is now looking his way.

"It depends on what you mean by private," says the minotaur. "If you mean a soundproof room with two-way glass and a camera to record every detail of what you say in response to my questions, then yes, follow me."

"You're bringing me in for questioning?" says Klaus. "Why?"

"This morning I saw you attempting to enter the scene of the crime, and you were caught on camera around the museum, not long after the sponge was stolen."

"That's because I'm investigating the theft," says Klaus. "Come on, you know me, Darka."

"And you know me." Darka offers the handcuffs to Klaus. "I'd rather you came in willingly, but I'll cuff you and drag you in if necessary."

"Let's be sensible here," says Klaus. "You know I didn't take the Time Sponge."

Chief Inspector Darka snorts and flares his nostrils. "What I know –" he speaks in a hoarse whisper – "is that my ghoul forensic team found a strand of yeti hair on the plinth where the sponge was resting."

"I… " Klaus is floundering. You're so used to seeing him in control of any given situation. He seems flustered. It's warm inside the precinct and a number of the other officers and criminals are watching the unfolding scene with interest. "Oh, I get it. Night Mayor Franklefink is breathing down your neck to make an arrest, isn't he? He wants to make it look like he's being tough on crime so you're setting me up."

You get the feeling that Klaus is scrabbling about for a reason, but he must have touched on a sensitive subject because Chief Inspector Darka's expression darkens. "I don't think you want to be throwing around wild theories like that, Solstaag. Your options are to come quietly or be forcibly arrested."

Klaus sighs. You're surrounded by UPF officers who will jump to it if their chief gives the word. "All right, Darka. I'll answer your questions."

Klaus turns, smiles at you and mouths, "I won't be long," before following Darka into the room.

The door swings shut and the centaur desk sergeant looks at you over his glasses.

"The waiting room is that way."

He points to the door Gretchen went through.

You hesitate, unsure what to do.

"Or the exit is there," he adds. "Your choice."

? Wait for Klaus in the waiting room.

Turn to page 184
THE WAITING ROOM

? Or leave and see what you can find out without him.

Turn to page 133
A WITCHY TIP

A WITCHY TIP

IT'S OVERCAST AND CHILLY OUTSIDE, but you're relieved to get out of the station. You step into the street and shiver. In spite of the cold, your armpits are hot and clammy. You feel more vulnerable than you did on the way in and you can sense the panic surging through your veins. Without Klaus to protect you, you're acutely aware of the criminal eyes that watch your every step. There are werewolves, ogres, trolls and goblins and they all have the scent of human in their nostrils.

You take a deep breath and try to calm yourself. Klaus hasn't been arrested. Not yet. They will probably release him in an hour or so. But what if they don't? And what about the yeti hair they found? *What if...* You can barely bring yourself to think it... What if Klaus really did commit this crime? You hate this feeling of doubt. Surely you can trust your boss.

The thoughts that swirl around your mind make you feel dizzy. You close your eyes, trying to think clearly. When you open them, you're staring into the faces of a pair of wrinkly wart-ridden witches who you know all too well.

"Confused?" says Bridget Milkbird.

Wisps of magical smoke vanish into the air.

"Confused and all alone," says her sister, Burnella.

"Just like Klaus's previous assistant was before he fell down that bottomless pit," says Bridget.

The witches cackle with laughter.

"I'm sure that won't happen to you, though," says Bridget. "I'll bet you've already worked out who took it, haven't you? We've seen you taking notes. Who is it, then?"

You keep your lips sealed, but you almost jump out of your skin when Burnella magics herself next to you. She is trying to peer over your shoulder and take a look at your notebook. You clutch it to your chest.

"Oh, suit yourself. And to think we were going to tell you how to summon the lobster," says Burnella.

"Were we?" says Bridget. "Why would we do that?"

"Out of the kindness of our hearts?" suggests Burnella.

"We haven't got any hearts. We swapped them for a couple of magic cabbages. Remember?" says Bridget.

"Oh, that's right. Turned out they weren't magic at all."

"That's right. Mine's gone mouldy too."

"Yes," says Burnella, "and since we have mouldy cabbage hearts there's no reason for us to point out that Bernard the time-bending lobster can be summoned by tearing a page in the book that he wrote. It disrupts the waves of time, forcing him into the present."

Bridget looks at her sister and shakes her head. "I thought we weren't going to help."

"Oh, sorry."

"Never mind your mouldy cabbage heart. It's your manky turnip brain that's the problem!"

"How dare you! Anyway, it's only useful information if you have a copy of the lobster's autobiography."

"True. Now, we'd better get back to our day job."

In a second puff of smoke, the sisters vanish, leaving you alone with your thoughts. You wonder how much use it would be to talk to Bernard anyway. If he knew who took the Time Sponge, surely he would have tracked them down himself. But time-bending lobsters are mysterious by nature and contacting Bernard might be your best chance of clearing Klaus's name.

A horn beeps. You recognize the sound immediately. Watson is waiting by the curb, panting happily. You open the passenger door and climb in.

? If you took the book, then you can reach into the glove compartment and get it.

Turn to page 137
BERNARD THE TIME-BENDING LOBSTER

? If you didn't take it then you need Watson to drive you back to the library.

Turn to page 170
DROUBLE TROUBLE

BERNARD THE TIME-BENDING LOBSTER

THE DOOR SLAMS SHUT AND Watson starts moving. You quickly yank the seatbelt over your shoulder. Until today you've only ever been in the car when Klaus is behind the wheel. Watson driving himself is much scarier.

The DJ Nick Grimm is talking on the radio. "And now, more on our unfolding news story regarding the missing Time Sponge and the recent report that Chief Inspector Darka is looking to question Private Investigator Klaus Solstaag. *News of the Unusual* reporter Gretchen Barfly-Sewer has more on this story."

You hear the banshee reporter's shrill voice.

"Yes, a few minutes ago, in dramatic scenes at the UPF station, Chief Inspector Darka cuffed, restrained and dragged the former police officer into a cell. It seems Klaus Solstaag has found himself on the wrong side of the law that he once enforced."

You reach forwards and switch it off. You don't need to hear Gretchen's exaggerations and lies. You need to learn the truth.

You take out Bernard's book. Leafing through it, you see that the pages are still blank. You take the corner of one of the pages between your fingers. It feels wrong. This book doesn't belong to you. You stole it. If you tear a page, perhaps the lobster will appear and maybe he'll help you, but what if he doesn't? What if he refuses to help? What if he's annoyed that you tore his book? Is a time-bending lobster a thing to fear? Only here on the Shady Side of Haventry would you find yourself seriously asking questions like these.

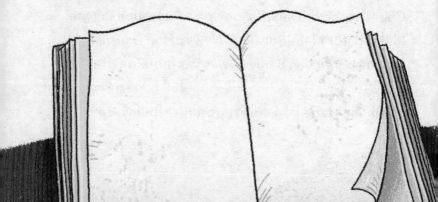

Watson suddenly swerves to the left, over the pavement and on to Snark Park, the patch of overgrown land at the centre of Haventry's Shady Side. Before you took the job, you would never have considered entering, but Watson gives you no choice.

You're still clutching the book as you cross the bumpy grass into a dark wooded area. You have heard that all kinds of terrible creatures lurk in these woods. You have no idea why Watson is taking you here until he comes to a screeching halt. You feel the tug of the seatbelt and see why he's stopped.

You're in front of Lake Stench, in the middle of Snark Park. Its water is brownish grey. A light mist hangs over it, obscuring the occasional eye or tentacle that breaks the surface of the water. Many strange things lie within.

Watson turns off his engine. You understand what you have to do. He's brought you to water, and where else would you expect to find a lobster? It's time to tear the paper. You make a tiny rip and instantly the pages ripple and flicker. The book vibrates, then it springs from your hands and lands in the footwell of the car. You look down at it and see that words are appearing on every page. The pages are moving too fast to read. You reach down to grab it but the book flaps its covers and flies out of the open car window. You watch helplessly as it dives into the water with an almighty *SPLASH!* You jump out of the car and run to the water's edge.

Slowly, something rises up out of the lake. Two waving antennae, a pair of large claws and six wiggling legs. It hovers in front of you.

"I am Bernard the time-bending-lobster! Who is it that summons me?"

You're too astonished to reply. Luckily, he isn't waiting for an answer.

"I already know, of course. We have been here before, you and I."

You have no idea what he means.

"Everything that happens to me in the present has already happened in the past and is yet to happen in the future. Such is the nature of those of us who understand that time is not a road to walk down but an ocean through which one must swim. Yes, I am Bernard the time-bending lobster."

You're beginning to wonder if summoning this lobster is actually going to prove useful. So far, he just keeps introducing himself.

"As I have witnessed this moment before, I already know why you are here. You are working with the detective I hired to find the Time Sponge."

As the lobster speaks, the world around you wobbles. Your surroundings aren't as solid or real as you thought. You are unsure what is happening. You feel lightheaded.

"I hired your boss, but it is you, his assistant, who will take hold of the sponge. Maybe you already knew that? Only you know what you know and you'll never know what I know ... if you know what I mean?"

You're doing your best to follow what the lobster is saying but you are distracted by its swaying antennae and the way they make the air ripple and shimmer.

"I have seen all your possible futures but the present question is what you do next. You are torn, I can tell. So let me show you the two paths before you. You can return to the police station to try to help Klaus, or continue with the investigation and go to the museum."

A vision appears in the water. You see yourself entering the police station. With a ripple, the picture changes. This time, you're sneaking into the museum.

"Whatever you decide, we will meet again. When you find the Time Sponge I will return. Until then, goodbye!"

The lobster splashes back into the lake and you hear Watson's engine start up. You run back to the car and hop in. He switches into reverse and pulls away from the lake. His wheels skid in the mud, then he pauses. He's waiting to hear where you want to go next.

? Do you decide to return to the police station?

Turn to page 144
THE WRONG SIDE OF THE LAW

? Or do you think you should go to the museum?

Then turn to page 162
MARKETING GENIUS

THE WRONG SIDE OF THE LAW

YOU HAVE TO WAIT A while to see Klaus but finally
the centaur officer leads you to the visiting room.
Klaus sits in front of you, behind a window. Judging
by the scratch marks and bullet dents, it must be
re-enforced glass and it's obviously seen its fair
share of action. Klaus picks up a phone and motions
for you to do the same. When he speaks, his voice
comes through the earpiece.

"I haven't been formally charged yet – just brought
in for questioning," he says. "I'm pretty sure that this is
all theatrics, designed to show me they're serious.
They want me to slip up. That's why they let you see me.
This whole place is bugged. Just let me do the talking."

You nod.

"The only evidence they have is this hair of mine found at the scene of the crime and anyone could have found one of those and planted it there to set me up."

Sharing an office with your boss, you are certainly aware of how much white hair he sheds. But who would want to set him up? It's a good question but you keep it to yourself.

"Reading between the lines, I think Night Mayor Franklefink has been breathing down his neck, but Darka is embarrassed that it was stolen while he was guarding it. I need some information to use as leverage to get myself out of here."

Your eye catches a blinking light coming from a small camera pointed directly at you. Klaus is right that every word is being recorded. Every move is being watched. You have things you need to share but you bite your tongue.

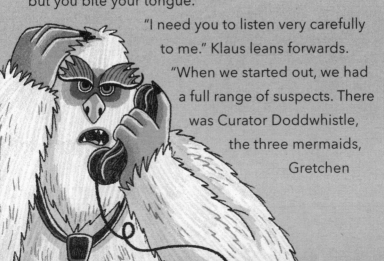

"I need you to listen very carefully to me." Klaus leans forwards. "When we started out, we had a full range of suspects. There was Curator Doddwhistle, the three mermaids, Gretchen

Barfly-Sewer and Professor O'Leary."

You notice that he doesn't mention Chief Inspector Darka or DS Rigmarole in that list. It makes sense, since Klaus knows this conversation isn't exactly private.

"But what if we overlooked someone?" He leans forwards. "Someone a little closer to the scene of the crime," he says under his breath. "And I don't mean Doddwhistle."

He's talking about the police, but he obviously isn't as subtle as he thinks because suddenly the door behind him swings open and the huge minotaur chief lumbers into the room. The clip-clop of his footsteps is so loud that the phone squeaks with feedback. Darka scowls at you. His breath steams up the window with condensation. He wipes it away with his gloved hand.

"Having a nice chat, are we?" he says.

You try to smile to disguise your fear. Chief Darka terrifies you. You're relieved when Klaus answers. "You and I both know that you can't hold me forever."

"You mean, unless I charge you?" says Darka, one of his bullish eyes still watching you. "And this is one old bull you don't want charging you!"

"Come on, Darka," says Klaus. "We go way back, you and me. You know I'm more use to you on the outside. I can help."

"You *have* helped," says Darka. "Klaus Solstaag, I am hereby arresting you on suspicion of the stealing the Time Sponge. You have the right to talk but anything you do say will be probably be ignored. You're officially on the wrong side of the law."

"I didn't do it," insists Klaus.

"Remember how we used to laugh whenever people said that?" says the minotaur. "Not so funny when you're the one saying it, is it? I'll tell you what, let's have one last little chat about ways to resolve this. Your friend can wait outside."

Klaus looks at you. "It's down to you now. You know that, don't you? I can't solve it while I'm locked up."

Chief Inspector Darka is also watching you, reading your every expression. "If I were you, I'd get out of here before we find a reason to drag you into this mess."

You do as he says, getting up and walking out as fast as your feet will carry you. You leave the room and return to the bustling precinct, where you almost bump into DS Rigmarole coming the other way. She's in such a hurry that she doesn't even notice you as she rushes along the same corridor you just walked down.

Your nerve endings are jangling. You feel the excitement of closing in on your suspect. Klaus was right. The answer lies with someone much closer to the theft, an officer of the law. But which one?

? Do you think it was Chief Inspector Darka?

Turn to page 149
DARKA ENLIGHTENS

? Or do you think Rigmarole stole the Time Sponge?

Turn to page 175
RIGMAROLE'S ROLE

DARKA ENLIGHTENS

WORKING ON THE SHADY SIDE of Haventry, you know there's no such thing as an ordinary case, but this one has felt different even by your usual standards. You've never before suspected that your own boss could be involved. You still wonder why he couldn't have been straight with you from the start but, as he always tells you, everyone has a secret. The trick is to work out who is lying about what.

You've been scrabbling around for a thread all day, trying to find one strong enough to pull on, but the harder you tug at them, the more easily they snap. It brings to mind something else Klaus said. *The simplest solution to a locked-room mystery is that it was the person with the key.*

You know that Chief Inspector Darka had one. From the first moment you encountered the minotaur police chief, he's tried to make you and your boss step away from the case. He clearly respects Klaus's detective skills so why keep him at arm's length? Surely Darka would want the crime solved?

Unless he was responsible for it.

You need to find out if your hunch is right. Head down, hands in pockets, you stride through the bustling police precinct. The centaur desk sergeant glances up at you. He's about to speak when he's distracted by a zombie with a gaping hole in his stomach.

"Oh great," says the officer. "You had to spill your guts all over my floor, didn't you?"

You use the moment and slip through the door that leads into the back of the station. There are cells and interview rooms along one end of the corridor and offices along the other.

You find a door with a sign saying: *CHIEF INSPECTOR DARKA.* You peek through the window. The room is empty. You turn the handle and slip inside, closing the door behind you as quietly as possible.

A fly buzzes around the office. Its movements are erratic and random but yours must be precise and focused.

Chief Inspector Darka's desk is a mess, with paper strewn everywhere. It reminds you of Klaus's office. You search through the piles of police reports, detailing all of the incidents recorded daily by the UPF officers. There are interviews with vampires about missing people, werewolves convicted of breaking into fried chicken shops and gnomes accused of trespassing in gardens. There's so much, but you don't find anything relevant.

You're reaching for a drawer handle when a silhouette appears at the frosted glass. From the outline of the horned head, you recognize it as Chief Inspector Darka. The only available hiding place is under the desk. There's no time to consider the wisdom of your decision. You drop to your knees and crawl into the space between the chair and the back of the desk as the minotaur enters the office.

You hear the sound of the blinds being drawn. The room darkens. What has he to hide? Has he seen you? You're curled up into a ball, preparing yourself for the sudden appearance of a furious bull-headed police chief. To your relief, he sits down at his desk. But the relief turns to fear as he pulls his seat in and slides his legs under the desk. His huge shins are millimetres from your nose. You hold your breath because you're terrified – and because his feet smell.

He opens a drawer and takes something out. Frustratingly, from this angle you can't see what it is. He closes the drawer then clicks a button on the desk phone. You hear the dialling tone followed by a series of beeps as he punches a number in. It rings a couple of times then a voice answers.

"Yes?"

"I have good news," says Darka.

"Oh, please don't tell me you've found the Time Sponge." You recognize the voice as belonging to Night Mayor Franklefink. "Every day that museum remains closed brings us closer to my dream shopping mall."

"I know, but—"

Franklefink interrupts. "Curator Doddwhistle's attempts to entice people into her sorry excuse for a museum are looking increasingly desperate. Museums are things of the past. My new mall will bring voters – sorry, customers – flocking. They have one here in Transylvania and it's the hub of the community."

"Which is all very interesting," says Darka, "but I was referring to our other conversation, the one about getting the crime rates down."

"Yes, good. I pledged to come down hard on crime. What is your plan?"

"The fact is…" Darka lowers his voice, "none of these officers are up to the job. I need better people."

"So you're suggesting we employ more UPF officers?"

"One more," says the chief.

"Do you have someone in mind?"

"Klaus Solstaag. As much as I hate to admit it, we lost our best officer when he left the force. We need him back."

"But he's freelance now, isn't he? Would he come back?"

"I think I may have found a way to entice him," says Darka.

You feel sudden panic in the pit of your stomach.

If Klaus went back to work for the UPF you would have to return to your ordinary life. You would no longer have an excuse to explore all the unusual goings-on in the Shady Side of Haventry.

A knock on the door interrupts the phone conversation.

"Sorry, chief," you hear the centaur officer say. "We have a situation with a pixie refusing arrest!"

"Honestly," snarls Darka. "Do I have to do everything around here? Franklefink, I'll call you later."

"Very well," says Franklefink. "And remember, we're in no hurry to find that sponge."

"Oh, don't worry. It won't be found for a while. You'll get your shopping mall."

Darka ends the call, slams the drawer shut and gets up. Once he's out of the room, you crawl out from under the desk and peek over the top to ensure that the coast is clear. You open the drawer and see a velvet drawstring bag. Cautiously, you pick it up, your hands shaking with nervous excitement. You pull it open and see a sponge. You tip the sponge into your hand and give it a cautious little squeeze.

WHOOAAAASHHHH!!!!

And just like that, the world stops turning. It isn't silence that fills the air. Every word that was being spoken, every creak, every beep or click is elongated into one continuous note. The sponge is glowing brightly through the gaps in your fingers.

You notice a small black dot hanging in the air in front of you. It's the trapped fly, frozen mid-flight. With your other hand, you reach up and touch it. Suddenly, it reanimates, buzzing around the room again. You realize that this must be how the sponge works. Everyone except you is frozen, but you're able to wake them up with a touch of your hand.

You continue to the door and along the corridor back to the main precinct. When you enter the room your jaw drops. No one is moving. It's eerie. It's as though the world is holding its breath. The desk sergeant is holding a mop. You decide to avoid looking at the mess he's clearing up. Chief Inspector Darka appears to be in the middle of yelling at a pixie. No one so much as wobbles.

You can hear the fly buzzing down the corridor behind you. You close the door on the precinct, fearful that the fly might escape and collide with any of these officers or criminals, awakening them from their frozen state.

The thought occurs to you that it isn't just the office. By holding the sponge, you've paused the entire world. It's a dizzying thought. Too much to comprehend. When you release the sponge, they will carry on without knowing that anything happened.

The feeling of power is overwhelming, but you need to stay focused. You find the cells and locate Klaus. DS Rigmarole is standing in front of him, holding a set of keys. She appears to be in the middle of saying something. Moving as slowly and as carefully as you can, you take the keys from her, knowing that one slip could jolt her out of her trance. You let out a sigh of relief when you have the keys in your hand. You find the right one to unlock the cell door. It creaks open but no one hears. You step up to your boss and tap his arm.

Just like the fly, Klaus suddenly awakens. He blinks and looks at you, then takes in his surroundings – the open cell door, the frozen elf on stilts and the sponge in your hand.

"Nicely played," he says. "I knew you'd figure it out. I'm guessing you found it in the chief's office."

You nod, relieved to have Klaus back. As you follow him back into the precinct, you realize this is how it always feels. It's always you and the yeti making your way through this crazy mixed-up world, trying to find the cracks in everyone's lies. You feel guilty about doubting him. Did you really suspect him of taking the sponge?

Klaus examines Chief Inspector Darka up close. Even the spittle from his mouth has frozen in the air. It's as beautiful as it is disgusting.

Klaus taps him on the arm.

"… or I will rip off your wings and—" yells the chief. "Solstaag… What? Oh."

Darka glances around. His eyes move down to your hand, still clutching the sponge. You take a step back but you have to be careful not to brush against any more of these police officers. "I see what's going on here," says Chief Darka.

"So do I," says Klaus. "I see this whole thing. You locked me up for a crime I didn't commit, then promised me you could make this whole thing go away if I came back to work for you."

Chief Inspector Darka flares his bullish nostrils and snorts but he doesn't deny it.

"I need you back, Klaus," he snaps.

"So much so that you were willing to break the law and frame an innocent yeti? I'll bet you placed that hair there yourself," says Klaus.

"You're making it sound worse than it is," says the chief. "I would have seen the sponge returned to its rightful owner eventually."

"To me, Bernard the time-bending lobster."

You hear this voice clearly, but neither Klaus nor the chief react. It is in your head. You can hear it because you hold the sponge. Such is its power.

"So what now, Solstaag?" snarls Darka.

"You mean, am I going to let everyone know that you stole the very thing you were supposed to be protecting and then tried to blackmail the best officer who ever worked for you?" asks Klaus.

"Something like that," says Darka sheepishly.

"The answer is no. I'm not going to expose your attempt to set me up, or let everyone know that you stole the sponge precisely for that purpose. But nor am I ever coming back."

You breathe a sigh of relief. Chief Darka looks imploringly at Klaus. "Please. I … need you."

Klaus shakes his head. "I'm sorry, but I made my decision. I left. I have other responsibilities now." He winks at you. He's chosen you and you feel relieved. You should be surprised by his decision to let Darka off the hook, but you know your yeti boss well enough to understand that it's never about crime and punishment with him. For Klaus, it's all about the challenge of solving a puzzle.

"And you, in return, are never going to pull anything like this again," continues Klaus. "You need to have a little more faith in your officers. I might josh with Rigmarole but when my assistant froze time, she was just in the middle of telling me she'd realized it was you too."

"Rigmarole knows?" says Darka.

"Yes." Klaus nods solemnly. "She was asking me for advice."

"What did you tell her?"

"We didn't get that far," replies Klaus. "And now we don't have to. You can resolve it between yourselves, but if you want my advice, you'll think about giving her more responsibility. You have a good officer there. She'll help you clean up these streets."

"Thank you, Klaus," says Darka. You can tell he wants to say more but his pride won't allow it. "So what now?"

"Now, my assistant and I will make sure it gets back to its rightful owner."

"Bernard the time-bending lobster," says the voice in your head.

You drop the sponge into the velvet bag. In a matter of seconds, the world springs back to life. No one is aware that a moment ago they stood as static as statues. In fact, the only one not moving now is Darka, who watches you walk towards the door. Before you leave, you see Rigmarole appear from a doorway. She looks confused. After all, as far as she's concerned, Klaus was behind bars. Klaus gives her a little wave.

"I wonder what he'll tell Rigmarole," says Klaus. "Will he admit the truth? Hopefully. He made a mistake. We all do that from time to time. Let's hope he learns from it."

You follow Klaus out of the station into the street. You're pleased to be following again, but you still have the bag in your hand. Klaus hasn't yet asked you to hand it over. You feel the weight of the sponge. The urge to take it out again is overwhelming. After all, no one would know. All you have to do is drop it into your hand and you can take another moment to yourself.

"Yes. The time is NOW," speaks the voice.

You open the bag, reach in and grab the sponge. Everything stops.

YOU HAVE REACHED ONE OF THE THREE POSSIBLE ENDINGS.

Turn to page 217
THE END?

MARKETING GENIUS

INVESTIGATING WITHOUT KLAUS, YOU'VE NEVER felt
so alone in your life. Every decision you've made
has been entirely down to you. Every action that
led you here to the Museum of Magical Objects
and Precious Stones was yours. Klaus is being held
by the UPF. Watson is waiting on a single yellow
line. It is you – and you alone – who must do what's
necessary to solve this crime.

You're in the museum and you just heard
footsteps. There's a grandfather clock outside the
exhibit room. You open the front panel and sneak
inside, pulling the door shut just in time. You can
hear voices. Curator Doddwhistle and DS Rigmarole

enter the exhibit room, mid-discussion. You spy on them through the keyhole.

"I don't really understand why you've asked me here. You're wasting police time." Rigmarole sounds furious.

"I have asked you here, my dear, because I want you to call it off," replies Curator Doddwhistle.

"Call what off?"

"The investigation."

"Why would you want to call off the investigation? We haven't found the Time Sponge yet."

"OK, not call off, but … let's just say, there's no rush," says Curator Doddwhistle. "I'm sure it will turn up sooner or later."

"But … but … but," stammers Rigmarole. "I thought the museum needed to reopen."

"It is reopening, my dear."

You shift to get more comfortable, but it's cramped inside the clock and you can feel your leg going to sleep. Curator Doddwhistle and DS Rigmarole are standing in the centre of the room. Doddwhistle has removed her woollen hat and the ancient snakes on her head are slithering around.

"I'm confused," says DS Rigmarole. "I thought the Time Sponge was the centrepiece of the exhibition."

Doddwhistle places a hand on the empty plinth. "It was. It is certainly a big attraction. And its disappearance was a stroke of marketing genius."

"Marketing genius?" repeats Rigmarole.

"So it seems. I almost wish I had stolen it. The *News of the Unusual* and Shady Side Radio have been running the story all day. They've been calling it a locked-room mystery and the public do love a good mystery. The phone hasn't stopped ringing."

"You mean you're reopening the time-travel exhibition without it?"

Doddwhistle peels off the label above the Memory Basin and hands it to Rigmarole. "No.

We're not reopening the time-travel exhibition. Welcome to our brand new 'Locked-Room Mystery'. Our visitors are invited to gather all the evidence and try to solve the mystery themselves. It's proving very popular and it's already booked out for a fortnight."

She carefully sticks another label in its place, then attaches more signs around the room.

"Personally, I rather fancy Professor O'Leary as a prime suspect. The mermaids were back at their hotel during the time of the theft so it looks like it wasn't them. But it doesn't really matter what I think. This place hasn't been so popular since 1895 when we got all that cursed Egyptian stuff in." Curator Doddwhistle sounds upbeat. "The yummy mummies loved that." She stoops to pick up the broken bowl of cookie dough.

"You really shouldn't move... Hold on, that wasn't knocked over before. This is completely irregular. You can't touch anything and you certainly can't let the public in," says Rigmarole.

"It's my museum and I'll do what I want," replies Curator Doddwhistle. "I have to get my new exhibition ready for the grand opening. It's going to be enticing, intriguing and ... experiential." Her eyes brighten and the decrepit snakes on her head hiss.

"But ... but ... you're talking about selling tickets to a crime scene," argues Rigmarole. "Chief Darka won't be happy."

"That's true," admits the curator. "But he's one of the main suspects. After all, he had the key." She shows Rigmarole to a corner of the room with a set of keys and a screen showing several enlarged fingerprints. Above this is a picture of Inspector Darka with the word *SUSPECT* written across it.

In spite of her obvious disapproval it's clear that Rigmarole is intrigued by the display. She leans over to take a closer look. "What about the spare key in your room?" she asks.

"That's a very good point," says Curator Doddwhistle. "I should have a display for that one too."

"A display!" Rigmarole snaps. "Criminal cases should be solved by professionals, not by amateurs and certainly not by nosy members of the public."

"Yes, except in this case, the professionals are all on the suspect list." Doddwhistle presses a button and a panel opens up to reveal a poster with photos and lots of arrows pointing to various clues. It reminds you of your own notes.

"You made a crime board?" exclaims Rigmarole. "How dare you?" Rigmarole's voice grows higher and squeakier the angrier she gets.

"Oh, calm down, dear. You'll fall off your stilts." Curator Doddwhistle mops up the spilled cookie dough and wrings it into the bowl. "Now, I don't want to waste any more of your valuable police time, Detective Inspector."

"I'm a Detective Sergeant."

"That's funny, I could have sworn I read *inspector* in the Fortune Cookie Dough."

"Really?" Rigmarole's eyes light up at the idea of a promotion.

They're both leaving the room. You hold your breath as they pass.

"Yes, but it's not terribly reliable." Curator Doddwhistle pauses at the door. "Talking of which, next time you see your boss—"

"Chief Darka?"

"No, I meant the big boss, Night Mayor Franklefink. Tell him he'll have to wait a little longer to open that mall. This museum is open for business." A warm smile spreads across her face.

"I don't work for the Night Mayor," says Rigmarole. "Politicians come and go. Law and order is all I care about."

You hear a hiss from Doddwhistle's snakes. "That's good to hear," she says. "But my concern is my museum and, right now, I have to get it ready."

Rigmarole looks like she wants to say more but she bites her lip and leaves. Curator Doddwhistle trots along the corridor and disappears up the stairs that lead to her office.

You push the panel door and climb out, but as you

do you notice something sticking out
from under the clock. A green fountain pen.
You pick it up and examine it, wondering if you aren't
the only one who's hidden inside the clock recently.
On the side is printed: *SHADY SIDE UNIVERSITY*.

You slip the pen into your pocket and hurry along
the corridor. You sneak out of the back door, being
careful to avoid the gargoyles that oversee the back of
the building. Once you reach a safe distance, you catch
your breath. Watson is waiting for you by the curb,
panting. He can sense it too: the end is near. It's time to
decide. Who do you think stole the Time Sponge?

? Do you think that DS Rigmarole was acting
suspiciously just now?

Turn to page 175
RIGMAROLE'S ROLE

? Or perhaps you think Chief Inspector Darka is the
one who took the sponge?

Turn to page 149
DARKA ENLIGHTENS

? Or does something now make you think it was
Professor O'Leary?

Turn to page 190
THE GIFT OF THE PRESENT

DROUBLE TROUBLE

CONSIDERING HOW LONG WATSON HAS been a car now, he doesn't seem overly familiar with the rules of the road. He's taking you to the library but, as you clutch the sides of your car seat, you wonder whether he'll get you there in one piece. He hurtles the wrong way down a one-way street. Horns beep and drivers shout rude words as he makes his way across town. At one point, he spots a cat and mounts the pavement. Panicked, you grab the steering wheel and bring him back on to the road.

When you finally arrive outside the library you feel relieved … and a bit sick. The door opens and you step out. You pat Watson on the bonnet, grateful that he's brought you where you need to be and that you didn't lose your life (or your lunch) in the process.

You can hear Drouble the two-headed guard dog barking as you approach. He's seen Watson. A plan quickly formulates in your head. Drouble likes Watson but his lead is attached to the desk so all you have to do is get inside, untie him, then make sure Watson gives him a long enough run-around to allow you to get into the library and grab the book.

Your legs turn to jelly as you approach the two sets of razor-sharp teeth.

You push open the door and the barking changes to a low, threatening growl. Drouble has picked up your scent. You remember what Professor O'Leary said about the library not being open to humans. You're so accustomed to having Klaus by your side, sometimes you take for granted the protection he provides. Without him, there's nothing to prevent this enormous two-headed dog from biting chunks out of you with both of its mouths.

Watson's horn sounds and both of Drouble's heads look up eagerly, his tongues flapping out the sides of his mouths like a pet dog waiting for a ball to be thrown. Watson revs his engine and swishes his windscreen wipers.

He's showing Drouble that he wants to play. Drouble appears to forget all about you as he strains against his lead. You seize the moment and run to the wall, where you unclip the lead. Drouble is free.

However, there's another problem. The library entrance is a revolving door and its chambers are too small for a dog of Drouble's size to get through. He growls and whines as he tries to get his right head into one chamber and his left one into another. Outside, Watson does a little wheel-spin.

You notice a second door beside the revolving one. It opens inward so you grab the bar and pull. Drouble pays you no attention but when he sees the door open, he bolts, chasing after Watson, who is already speeding down the road.

Situations like this make you wonder how the Shady Side community manages to keep so many of its secrets, but you know that most who do witness this bizarre event will assume that Drouble's heads belong to a pair of dogs running side by side, chasing a car.

Now is not the time to worry about it. You make your way through the library as fast as your legs will carry you. You find the shelf and grab the book. As you take it, you hear barking again.

Watson's back. There is no time to open the book, so you get moving. As you reach the entrance you can see Drouble happily chasing Watson around, trying to sniff his rear bumper. You step out of the library and wave at Watson. He comes to a sudden stop by the side of the curb. Drouble is confused by this, at first suspecting it might be a game. He nudges Watson's side door but Watson is once again acting like a car.

Disappointed, Drouble returns to the library, both heads lowered, both tails having lost their wag. He doesn't even glance at you. When you reach Watson, the door swings open. You jump in and the radio comes on.

"Breaking news," says Nick Grimm. "We're hearing

that Chief Darka, who has been questioning private detective Klaus Solstaag, is going to formally arrest the yeti for the theft of the Time Sponge."

Watson revs his engine. He wants to know where to go.

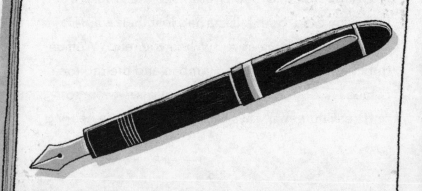

? Do you want to go back to the police station to help Klaus?

Turn to page 144
THE WRONG SIDE OF THE LAW

? Or should you tear a page from the book and summon Bernard?

Turn to page 137
BERNARD THE TIME-BENDING LOBSTER

RIGMAROLE'S ROLE

YOUR HEAD IS STILL SPINNING. This case has been a journey of discovery. Behind every closed door there seems to be another one, but you sense you're finally closing in on the truth. DS Rigmarole was the first person you met on your investigation. Now, she's your prime suspect. You just need to piece together the order of events and catch her out.

You're inside the bustling police precinct and you've found her desk, but she's not here. You're aware that you stand out, being neither police officer nor criminal, and although you feel tempted to look through the things on her desk, you don't want to end up behind bars, like your boss.

Noticing that Rigmarole has left her UPF jacket on the back of her chair and her hat on the desk, you act quickly. You slide your arms into the jacket and pull the hat down over your face. You're hoping no one noticed when you hear a voice behind you say, "Off your stilts, are you, Rigmarole?"

It is Chief Inspector Darka.

You nod, hoping he doesn't demand you turn to face him.

"Now you're back from the museum, you should go and keep the pressure on Solstaag," he says. "Remember, there's a lot riding on us finding the thief."

You aren't confident enough to try doing an impression of Rigmarole, so you grunt in reply, then you keep your head down as you walk through the precinct, terrified that at any moment the real Rigmarole might reappear. You can barely breathe, you're so scared. When you finally reach the door, you push it open and slip into the corridor. You find the cell where Klaus is being kept. Rigmarole is standing in front of him. She has her back to you. You dive under a desk. Rigmarole swings round to see who's entered but doesn't spot you. You exhale very slowly and as quietly as you can manage considering how hard your heart is pounding.

"Who's there?" says Rigmarole.

"It's no one," says Klaus.

Has he seen you? Is he covering for you? It's hard to tell but you're relieved when Rigmarole turns back to face him.

"It's OK. You can carry on gloating if you like."

"Gloat? Me?" replies Rigmarole. "Why? Because you're behind bars and I've just been made the lead investigator on the crime of the year?"

"Darka's made you lead investigator?" says Klaus. "Interesting. He really must not want this one solved."

"You can joke all you like," counters Rigmarole. "But the *News of the Unusual* is calling me the New Cop on the Block. I like that but I might have to talk to Gretchen about a nickname with a bit more staying power. After all, I'm not going anywhere."

"Oh."

You can't see Klaus's facial expression, but you're so attuned to the subtleties of his voice that you can tell from his *"Oh"* that he's found a thread to pull. He's homing in on his suspect too.

"And when you find the Time Sponge…" he says.

"And when I find it, I'll be the hero." Rigmarole smirks.

"And Darka still hasn't found a new detective inspector, has he? You'd be a shoo-in for the job."

Klaus speaks conversationally, trying to get Rigmarole to lower her guard. It seems to be working, judging by the way she leans against the bars, clearly enjoying being in control of the situation.

Klaus places a hand on a bar and leans in too, lowering his voice, but it's still loud enough for you to hear. "*Detective Inspector Rigmarole* has a nice ring to it."

You find an angle where you can see Rigmarole's face. She has a faraway look in her eyes as though imagining this version of the future. You can see Klaus's other hand moving. Is he going to grab her and try to escape? It's not clear.

"Of course," adds Klaus. "There's no guarantee of you finding the sponge but then, I guess that's just a detail. No one could expect you to be as

perfect as your predecessor."

Rigmarole looks him squarely in the eye. "Oh, but I *will* find it."

"I suppose that depends on where you look," says Klaus. "Also, sorry about the shove."

"What shove?" she asks.

"This one." Klaus jabs his left hand through the bars and pushes Rigmarole. She's caught off guard and tumbles over. As she falls, something flies from the top of one of her stilts.

"Catch it!" Klaus yells, and you realize he means you. He *did* spot you when you entered and now he needs your help. A small velvet bag is hurtling towards you.

You dart out from under the desk and grab it. As your fingers close around the bag, you squeeze whatever is inside. Something glows and you feel as though someone is pouring treacle over you. The sponge is inside the bag and it's freezing time. You can see Klaus behind the bars and Rigmarole mid-fall, her body angled around as she tries to grab the sponge. But you've beaten her to it.

"You have it in your grasp," says a voice. "Time bends to your will."

The voice belongs to Bernard the time-bending lobster, the owner of the sponge.

To your astonishment, you see that everything has stopped. You look down at the bag clutched in your fist. You've paused time. Rigmarole is mid-fall. She must have been holding the cell keys because they're hovering in the air. You grab them, unlock the door, then release your grip on the sponge.

Time restarts.

"Yes!" Klaus punches the air in celebration. "Nice work."

"What the… How did… Oh, I see. " Rigmarole gets up but she's come off her stilts, making her the same height as you. "Remember that there are hundreds of officers on the other side of that door."

"And one thief on this side of it," says Klaus. "If I were you, I don't think I'd be in a rush to bring them in here. So, let's go through what happened, shall we?"

Rigmarole is looking around furiously, trying to work out how to play this but you've caught her red-handed with the Time Sponge and now Klaus is going to enjoy explaining how it came to be in her possession.

"Chief Inspector Darka was on guard last night but you were there too, weren't you? You were supposed to be guarding the outside, but you came in, didn't you? You were aware that Darka had drunk a lot of sparkling pop so you knew he'd have to visit the toilet. You simply waited until he was gone, then snuck in."

"Then how do you explain the locked door?" asks Rigmarole.

"Good question," says Klaus. "Darka would have taken the key but there's a spare in Doddwhistle's office. She doesn't see so well these days. I'm guessing you snuck in and took it at some point during the press night. That would mean you could go in and get the sponge, then hide it where no one was going to find it – in the space between your foot and the stilt. When we saw you outside the museum, one of your stilts rattled. I'll bet you couldn't connect it properly with the sponge hidden inside."

"You can't prove a thing," states Rigmarole, but you can tell from her tone that Klaus has guessed right.

"When we first started this investigation, we wanted to know why the thief took it. There are so many reasons why you would want it but the fact is, you didn't steal it to use it. You stole it so you could play the big detective hero who found it."

"I'm a good detective," snaps Rigmarole. "But Darka's never got over losing you. I borrowed the sponge because I wanted to convince him it was time to promote me, but I would never have let anyone else take the blame for it. Not even you."

"That's good to hear," says Klaus. He turns to you. "Well done. Now, let's get out of here. We'd better make sure this thing is returned."

"But … you won't tell, will you?" says Rigmarole. "Come on, Klaus. You and me go way back. And we're on the same side, here. We both want to make Haventry a safe place for everyone."

"The difference is that I'm not committing any crimes." He smiles. "But I can see your heart was in the right place. You're a good cop, Rigmarole. Not quite as good as I was but you'll get there." Klaus pauses, with his hand on the door handle. "I'll tell you what," he says, "if I walk out of here without any hassle I'll leave it to you to explain to Darka what happened. I don't care if you make out that you found it so long as you don't include me in your story."

"You'd do that for me, Klaus?" she says.

"My assistant and I solve mysteries. We'll leave the rest up to you."

You smile. Rigmarole looks relieved.

"I'll admit that you're not as bad as I thought," says Rigmarole.

"And you're better than you've been acting," replies Klaus, "but I can't trust you to return the Time Sponge to its rightful owner and I have a case to close."

"Thanks, Klaus. I owe you one," says Rigmarole.

"I'll remember that," replies Klaus.

You follow him through the door into the precinct.

"The time is NOW," says the voice of Bernard. "Squeeze the TIME SPONGE!"

The voice wants you to freeze time. You have already felt its effect fleetingly. You yearn to feel it again. You open the bag, reach in and grip the sponge.

YOU HAVE REACHED ONE OF THE THREE POSSIBLE ENDINGS.

Turn to page 217
THE END?

THE WAITING
ROOM

THE WAITING ROOM IS A stark contrast to the main police precinct. The noise and chaos is replaced by the peace and quiet of a chilly room with a large wooden fan turning slowly. A gnome wearing a suit and clutching a briefcase perches on a bench. Opposite him, a goblin grandmother sits eating a bag of toffees. Neither the gnome nor the goblin acknowledge you as you enter but the flame-haired banshee in the corner looks up from her phone and smiles.

"Ah, Klaus Solstaag's latest assistant," says Gretchen Barfly-Sewer. "Take a seat. It must have come as quite a shock to learn that your boss is a thief."

You say nothing.

"You think he's innocent, don't you?" she says. "How sweet to remain loyal in such trying times. But you aren't sure, are you? What is it he always says? Everyone has a secret. Everyone lies."

The way she looks at you is unnerving. She's the only banshee you've ever met. You've heard that they have a terrible shriek that renders their enemies useless, but with Gretchen, this comes out as a high-pitched laugh that scratches your ears like razorblades. You try to block the sound with your palms but it's as though her voice has slipped inside your head. It's unbearable and when it stops you're overwhelmed with gratitude.

"Most can't stand the sound," she says. "Most will tell me anything to make it stop."

She laughs again and the pain returns. You want to cry out and plead with her, but you fight the urge.

"Hey, quit your screeching," says a police officer by the door.

She smiles and shrugs. "Sorry." She turns back to you. "My readers love a good story like this. We've printed twelve editions of the paper already today. A locked-room mystery, an object with incredible power, intrigue, deception. It's got it all, but how should things be resolved? What makes a satisfactory ending? Some readers like to guess who did it. Others want a nice juicy plot twist."

She laughs again. Her breath is as cold as ice. You feel the urge to tell her everything you're thinking. It's as though you've drunk a truth serum. You do your best to resist.

"All good journalists know how to tell a story. It's all about which facts you include and which you leave out. Take Ma Squelch there."

She stands up, then leans over you so that her words trickle into your ear like poison. She points at the goblin as she speaks.

"This poor grandmother has lots of mouths to feed and not enough money to do it with. She's here waiting to collect one of her grandsons. The poor thing was arrested for stealing an apple – because he was starving. It seems

so unfair, doesn't it? Your sympathies are with her."
Gretchen places a hand on your shoulder and
squeezes.

It is hard to resist the persuasive powers of the
banshee's voice. She moves around to your other
ear and continues.

"But what if I tell you that Ma Squelch is down
here every other day because she and her family are
always in trouble with the law? She hasn't enough
money for food because she spends it all at the
dragon races. Those toffees were snatched out of a
child's lunchbox earlier today and she doesn't even
know which grandson has been arrested. Suddenly,
you feel differently about her, don't you? Isn't it
wonderful being told how to think?"

To your horror you realize you're nodding in
agreement. You try to get a grip on yourself. You
blink and shake your head, desperate to free
yourself of the memory of her awful laugh.

"So what would make a good solution to the
mystery of the Time Sponge?" she says. "I've heard
the mermaids have been shoplifting all over town.
Maybe I should splash them all over the front page.
Would that sell papers, I wonder?" She wrinkles her
nose as she ponders the question.

Is that all this is to her? A way to sell papers and manipulate people? She doesn't care about the truth at all. Not like you.

"What about Curator Doddwhistle? She's certainly got secrets but everyone knows the museum is in trouble. And is it any wonder? It's so old-fashioned, it's like a museum of what museums used to be like. The sooner they tear it down, the better, I say. Maybe she stole the sponge in some desperate attempt to draw attention to the old place. That theory is going down well with the readers. They'd much rather a smart shopping mall than a run-down old museum."

Her twitching lips and mischievous eyes reveal how much she's enjoying weaving her ideas inside your head. They're making you feel dizzy. You stare up at the slowly turning fan, rendered helpless by the terrible sound of Gretchen's laugh.

"There are other suspects of course," she says. "There are always others, aren't there? Perhaps you think *I* took it. I tell you, I wish I had. But yes, I shall probably find out it was the mermaids... Or Doddwhistle... Or maybe even your boss."

"Gretchen Barfly-Sewer," says the officer at the door. "We're ready for the press briefing now."

She stands up. "About time too."

Before walking out, she turns back to you.

"It's your decision what to do, though, of course."

The door closes behind her and you're suddenly free from her spell, but all her theories are still in your head. She's right: only you can decide what to do.

? Will you take Watson to look for the mermaids?

Turn to page 201
MERMAIDS AND MEMORIES

? Or will you tell Watson to drive you to the museum to see whether Gretchen is right about Curator Doddwhistle?

Turn to page 207
LOBSTER IN THE BASIN

? Or do you want to wait until you get a chance to speak to Klaus first?

Turn to page 144
THE WRONG SIDE OF THE LAW

THE GIFT OF THE PRESENT

YOU'RE GLAD YOU HAVE WATSON. As a dog, he can sniff out Professor O'Leary. As a car, he can also deliver you right to him.

You find the leprechaun lecturer strolling confidently along the pavement on the verge of Haventry's Shady Side. Here, the more extraordinary members of the community mix with everyone else. A few passers-by stop to stare at the tiny green-haired man in the large hat, but most assume he must be dressed up like that for some reason or other.

There's a lot of traffic on the road and cars are beeping at Watson for driving so slowly, so you get him to pull over and follow the professor on foot.

When he stops outside a glass-fronted building, you duck behind a tree. You peek around the trunk and see him walking up the steps to the entrance. You're shaking with nerves as you follow him. This won't be the first time you've closed in on a suspect, but you've never attempted it alone. You miss Klaus. You wish he was here but you'll just have to do your best.

Inside a sign reads: *GIANT LION PUBLISHING*. A human receptionist sits behind the front desk. These days, you almost feel more unnerved by these kinds of places than you do by police precincts run by minotaurs, museums run by gorgons or libraries guarded by two-headed dogs.

The man looks up at you and says, "Are you two together?"

This takes you off guard and confuses you. Then you feel a hand on your shoulder.

"My assistant and I have business here," says a familiar voice.

Even before you turn, you recognize the voice. Klaus is standing behind you, his large coat buttoned to the top, his hat pulled low. As far as the receptionist is concerned, this is a tall, white-bearded gentleman in a fur-lined coat. The idea of a real-life yeti walking into the building is too preposterous to consider.

"Do you have an appointment?" asks the receptionist.

"Yes, with Professor O'Leary. He's one of your authors. Short fellow. Big hat."

"Oh, that guy. He just went in. He's on floor twenty-one. You can take the lift."

"Thanks."

Klaus presses the button to call the lift. When it arrives, you follow him in. Once the doors have slid shut, he turns to you.

"Darka had to let me go," he explains. "That hair evidence wasn't strong enough and he knew it. He just thought he could make me sweat, but the only thing that makes this yeti perspire is when the air conditioning breaks. Once they let me go, I did a little digging and ended up drawing the same conclusion as you. Professor O'Leary was the one who took it. I don't know precisely *how* but I think I have an idea *why*. I'm guessing you do too. Let's go and find out if we're right."

The lift doors slide open. It's such a relief to have Klaus back by your side but you stop short of saying as much. You don't want him to know how anxious you felt while you were alone.

"Stride with purpose," says Klaus. "In my experience

you can walk through most places unnoticed if you stride with purpose."

You cross the open-plan office and find Professor O'Leary sitting in a glass-walled meeting room on his own. In front of him is a manuscript.

Hearing the door open, he speaks before looking up.

"I was thinking that maybe we can combine these two chapters, and I know what you mean about footnotes but…"

He stops when he sees that it isn't his editor who has entered the room.

"Ah, Klaus. I wasn't expecting to see you here. Have you written a book as well?" he asks.

"I'm more of a reader than a writer," says Klaus. "Talking of which, finished the book, then?" He leans over the desk to grab the manuscript. Professor O'Leary flips it over and places his elbows on it.

"It's a first draft, so it is. Very rough. The bulk of the work is still ahead of me, but yes, I have managed to sketch out a rough outline."

"If that's an outline then it's going to be quite a big book," says Klaus.

He's right. There must be a thousand pages in that pile of paper.

"Readers will certainly get their money's worth with this," replies Professor O'Leary smugly.

"In between all these public appearances, lectures and so on, I don't know where you find the time."

Klaus is goading him. He moves closer. Professor O'Leary is putting all his weight on the wad of paper, but Klaus is much stronger and easily picks it up in spite of the leprechaun's best efforts. He flips it over and reads the title.

THE GIFT OF THE PRESENT
By Professor Timothy O'Leary

"Neat title," says Klaus. "What's it about?"

"I don't really want to answer too many questions at this stage. Like I say, there's still a lot of work to do on it."

"Your first book was about the future, wasn't it?"

"*A History of the Future*, yes."

"And your second was about the past?"

"Yes, *The Future of the Past,* but..."

"And then you dried up," says Klaus.

"So I may have had a small problem with writer's block. What of it?"

Klaus picks up a pencil, holding one end in each hand. "So how did you get over it?" He snaps the pencil, making Professor O'Leary jump. Your boss has him right where he wants him. "You had an idea, didn't you? You remembered about the Time Sponge and realized it would give you the time to write your book. That's why you suggested that Curator Doddwhistle get the sponge for the exhibition." He points half a broken pencil at Professor O'Leary.

"Ah, well, no. To be sure, that's the wrong way around, so it is," says the professor. "I didn't even think of using it until I gave it a little squeeze while verifying that it really was the Time Sponge. But then, in that moment in the middle of that press conference, I knew what I had to do. I understood what a beautiful gift this object is. Can you imagine what it feels like to freeze time? It's incredible."

He's looking at you. Since you started on this case you've often imagined what it would feel like to squeeze the sponge. Even now, while the professor is confessing, you can feel its attraction. You desperately want to find it because you want to experience its power.

"So that's when you decided to steal the sponge," says Klaus.

"*Borrow*, not steal. And yes, but I also discovered I could use it as the subject matter of my book." He taps his manuscript proudly. "This is the first major work studying the present. It's about the nowness of now, the momentariness of every moment. It's a presentation of the present." His eyes light up. "I say, that's rather good, I should write it down."

He reaches for his pencil. Klaus hands him the two broken halves. "Why are you confessing now?"

"Isn't that obvious? I don't need it any more. It was always my plan to return it to the museum. It may as well be you who takes it back. The whole thing will come out anyway when the book is published." He places a small bag on the table and you already know the Time Sponge is inside. Your hand is drawn towards it.

"At the library, you told us about holding the Time Sponge

and seeing the raindrops pause in the sky. Except it didn't rain when you squeezed it at the press night yesterday... It rained this morning." Klaus makes the link at the same time you do. "You've been freezing time all day."

"Yes."

"But why? Why not just walk out with it during the press night, then return it before anyone even knew it was missing?"

"Because that was just one moment. I wanted to experience more. I even gave it a squeeze when we were in the library." Professor O'Leary chuckles. "It's such a peaceful place to write, especially when there's no danger of being disturbed." You recall how Professor O'Leary's bag seemed heavier on the way out of the library than it had on the way in. "As I often say, time travellers don't make the best writers, but those who can *pause* time are able to produce some wonderful prose, if I say so myself."

"So we have a why. Now for the how."

"Ah, the locked-room mystery," says Professor O'Leary.

"Not so hard to get around when you have the ability to freeze time, I suppose," says Klaus. "You certainly had enough time to work it out."

"I literally had time on my hands." Professor O'Leary chuckles, then tries to scribble down the thought. Unable to use the pencil, he pulls out a green fountain pen.

"Let me guess," says Klaus. "You took the spare key from Doddwhistle's office."

Professor O'Leary nods. "During that first squeeze during the press night, I strolled up to her office and borrowed the spare key. I placed the sponge back, then at the end of the event, I found a good hiding spot inside a grandfather clock by the door. When Darka went to the bathroom I snuck in and took the sponge."

He sounds delighted with himself.

"I'm guessing you left through the back door since Rigmarole was watching the front?"

"Yes, that's probably right. You'll have to forgive me if I forget the details. It was rather a long time ago."

"A long time ago?" echoes Klaus. "It only went missing last night."

"Last night for you," says Professor O'Leary. "I've spent months working on my book, while the rest of you were frozen in time. From my point of view, it was weeks ago that I saw you at the library. Anyway, you can take it back to the museum now. It hasn't even been missing for a day in real time. What harm have I done, really? Besides, Bernard already told me he won't press charges."

"What? But he—"

"Hired you? Yes, I know," said Professor O'Leary. "He told me."

"When?"

"The sponge and the lobster are linked. Whoever squeezes it is set adrift in the tides of time, where Bernard exists."

"Then why would he hire me if he knew you did it?"

"A good question." Professor O'Leary nods. "Being mysterious is very much in the nature of time-bending lobsters. It's what they do. But my guess is that at some point even further in the future he saw that he hired you so he hired you because he knew he was going to hire you."

"I'm not sure that makes sense," says Klaus.

"It makes perfect sense if you're a time-bending lobster, which is the one thing we can be certain of with Bernard," replies O'Leary. He turns to look at you. "I doubt you have the faintest clue what I'm talking about. Time travel is too complex for humans … and yetis, apparently." He gestures at the bag. "So are you going to take it or what?"

You reach for the bag, not stopping to ask yourself

whether he was talking to you or to Klaus. You grab it and peer inside. The contents looks like an ordinary yellow sponge, but you can feel its draw, its power.

"Are you feeling all right?" asks Klaus, turning to you.

You feel the weight of the sponge. You feel the temptation to give the bag a little squeeze. You want to experience its magic as well.

"This is your moment," says a voice. "I am Bernard the time-bending lobster." It echoes through your mind. "Take the sponge out and see the endless possibilities of this world."

You cannot resist the urge any longer. You squeeze the Time Sponge.

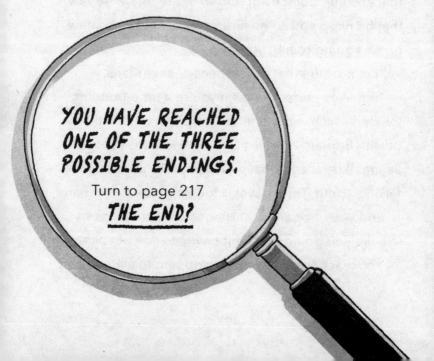

YOU HAVE REACHED
ONE OF THE THREE
POSSIBLE ENDINGS.
Turn to page 217
THE END?

MERMAIDS AND MEMORIES

YOU WALK DOWN THE STEPS of the police station to find Watson waiting obediently outside. You can tell he's disappointed that you're alone. You understand that. You miss Klaus too. You tell Watson that you want to find the mermaids. His engine starts with a bark and a growl. You plug in your seatbelt as he sets off but he only turns one corner before slamming on the brakes. You lurch forwards then rock back in your seat to see the reason he's stopped. You were leaving the station to find the mermaids, but they're here.

All three of them are in wheelchairs with blankets over their laps that barely hide their tails. A trio of hairy troll UPF officers are pushing them towards the station.

You pat Watson on the dashboard and step out of the car, as he swings the other door open and blocks the pavement. The troll officers come to a standstill.

"Please move out of the way," one of them grumbles.

The green-haired mermaid looks at you. "Have we met before? You look familiar."

"Sorry about her," says Annabelle. "Amelie has the same condition as the rest of us. Show the card, Fred."

"What card?" asks the male mermaid.

"This one." Annabelle pulls a card from under her blanket and holds it up.

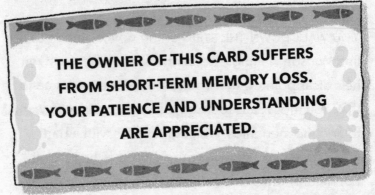

THE OWNER OF THIS CARD SUFFERS FROM SHORT-TERM MEMORY LOSS. YOUR PATIENCE AND UNDERSTANDING ARE APPRECIATED.

Annabelle puts the card away, then says. "Sorry. I can't find it."

"Find what?" asks Amelie.

"No idea," says Fred.

"These three are driving me round the twist," mutters one of the officers. "They were caught shoplifting but if I have to sit with them and fill out a report, I'll crack. I swear I will."

"Oh, is that what you're doing?" says Amelie. "I thought you were tour guides."

"I thought they were tour guides too," says Annabelle.

"I know a song about that," says Fred.

"Never trust a sea cow
To give a guided tour
Because they're very dull
And you'll step in their manure."

"No singing," says the troll behind him.

"Will all units please return to the station for an update on the museum theft," says a crackly voice from the troll's radio.

"There's been a theft at the museum?" says Annabelle. "We went there, didn't we?"

"Yes, we delivered the, er … what's it called?" says Amelie.

"What's what called?" asks Fred.

"The Time Sponge." Annabelle clicks her fingers. "That was it."

"Oh yes, I remember. Bernard's sponge thingy,"

says Amelie. "We brought it to the museum."

"Didn't someone steal that?" asks Fred.

The troll officers all shake their heads at each other despairingly.

"You lot were on the suspect list at first," says one of them, "but we checked with the hotel where you're staying, and it turns out you were back in the pool when the robbery took place."

"Were we?" asks Annabelle.

"Apparently so," says the troll. "The cuckoo clock on reception says you were singing rude songs all night."

"Ooh, I know a rude song," says Fred.

**"I knew a weak-bladdered mermaid
I think her name was Norma
And when you swam behind her
The water was much warmer."**

"I thought I said no singing," says the troll.

"Did you? I don't remember that," says Fred.

"If you ask me, it was that leprechaun professor," says Amelie.

"Oh, I remember him," agrees Annabelle. "Yes, he was very interested in it, wasn't he?"

"Who's very interested in what?" asks Fred.

"Someone in something," says Annabelle, losing the thread again.

"I think that gorgon … er, what's her name?" asks Amelie.

"Curator Doddwhistle," says a troll.

"That's it. I think she knows more than she's letting on."

"About what?" asks Fred.

"I can't remember," admits Amelie.

The troll officers give a sudden push and get the wheelchairs moving. Watson closes his door and you jump out of their way.

"What's happening now?" asks Annabelle.

"If we're going to get through this report with you, we'd better get started or it'll go on all evening," says the officer behind her.

"I think the tour is about to begin again," replies Amelie.

"That reminds me of a song I know," says Fred. "The tour was about to start, but I let out a f—"

"Come on," growl all three troll officers.

You watch as the mermaids are wheeled into the police station. Klaus is still in there and it isn't too late to go back and talk to him. Or would you rather carry on without him?

? Do you want to follow up on the mermaids' suspicions of Professor O'Leary?

Turn to page 190
THE GIFT OF THE PRESENT

? Or do you want to head back to the museum to see if you can find Curator Doddwhistle?

Turn to page 207
LOBSTER IN THE BASIN

? Or do you want to go and see Klaus after all?

Turn to page 144
THE WRONG SIDE OF THE LAW

LOBSTER IN THE BASIN

THE JOURNEY TO THE MUSEUM is as uneventful as any journey can be when it involves a car with the mind of a dog. You leave Watson outside the museum, with one wheel hitched up, leaking oil on a lamppost. You sneak into the museum, past the two gargoyles who watch the back of the building. One of them is asleep. The other is playing I-spy with a pigeon. Neither spots you.

You hurry along the corridor, past a large, ticking grandfather clock and into the display room. The plinth labelled *TIME SPONGE* is empty. The other exhibits remain. There's a bowl of gooey matter labelled *FORTUNE COOKIE DOUGH*. Across the room is *THE OCCASIONAL LAMP*, which flickers in and out of existence. But your eyes are drawn to *THE MEMORY BASIN*. Something is happening inside. The water swirls around. Cautiously, you reach out your hand and dip the tips of your fingers into the water.

It changes colour. It darkens and spits. A shape appears in the muddied liquid. It takes form and in the centre of the basin you see the image of a lobster.

"Greetings from the past," says the strange crustacean. "I am Bernard the time-bending lobster."

It's both captivating and a little unsettling. The lobster is looking directly at you.

"Yes, I see you," says the lobster. "As with all time-bending beings, I am connected to this basin and this basin is connected to me. The waters it contains are moved by the tides of time. I have seen you standing in this room. I have seen your hand, clutching my book. Whether this is in your past, present or future, I do not know. You seek that which has been lost and yet, to find it, you must not look to the past. The Time Sponge exists in the present. But you must now look to the future. Perhaps the Occasional Lamp can lead you to it, or else stirring the Fortune Cookie Dough."

You wonder why everything has to be so mysterious. Why can't someone just give you a straight answer occasionally?

? Should you touch the lamp?

Turn to page 213
THE OCCASIONAL LAMP

? Or stir the Fortune Cookie Dough?

Turn to page 210
THE FORTUNE COOKIE DOUGH

THE FORTUNE COOKIE DOUGH

You TAKE HOLD OF THE large wooden ladle sticking out of the bowl. The dough has solidified around it and you have to use both hands to stir. Slowly but surely the dough softens and you're able to stir faster. You stop and peer inside. The dough swirls around, then settles. Words appear:

TIME SPONGE FOUND:
THIEF REVEALED!
A GRETCHEN BARFLY-SEWER
EXCLUSIVE

The Fortune Cookie Dough tells the future. It's showing you that this mystery will be solved. The end is in sight. You grab the ladle and stir again. This time, it writes:

"IT WASN'T ME, TO BE SURE," CLAIMS THE THIEF

They sound like Professor O'Leary's words – and he is certainly on your list of suspects – but these are Gretchen Barfly-Sewer's headlines and you already know she's prone to lies and exaggerations.

You stir the dough again, hoping for more details.

EX-COP KLAUS CLEARS NAME

The relief you feel as you read his name makes you wish your boss was by your side now. You stir the dough again, but more vigorously this time. You steady the bowl, but your hand slips and it tips over. Its gooey contents splash out. You try to prevent it falling completely, but it too late. It crashes noisily to the floor.

You freeze, waiting to hear if anyone has heard. As you stand, rooted to the spot, you see that the spilled dough is forming a new sentence:

COULD IT BE CORRUPT COPPERS?
TIME WILL TELL

It's another one of Gretchen's headlines but, this time it seems to suggest that the police are behind the theft. Which version is true? Was the Time Sponge stolen by Professor O'Leary or the police?

Your thoughts are interrupted by the sound of approaching voices. Either you must find somewhere to hide or you need to get out. What do you want to do?

? Stay and hide?

Turn to page 162

MARKETING GENIUS

? Do you want to get back to Watson and look for Professor O'Leary?

Turn to page 190

THE GIFT OF THE PRESENT

? Or should you visit the police station?

Turn to page 144

THE WRONG SIDE OF THE LAW

THE OCCASIONAL LAMP

YOU REACH OUT YOUR TREMBLING hand. It seems strange, being this nervous about what looks like a very ordinary lamp but, just as your outstretched fingers are about to make contact with it, it flickers and vanishes. It was so solid. Now it's gone.

When it reappears you reach out to grab it but it disappears again and you're left clutching your own fist. You hover your hand over the place where it stood but you're nervous about what would happen if the lamp rematerialized in the space occupied by your hand.

You keep your palm millimetres away from where it stood and remain as steady as you can, focused on the task. When it appears, you quickly snatch it, half expecting to miss it again, so you're shocked when you feel cold metal between your fingers.

For a moment, nothing happens. Then, with a sudden sharp electric shock in your fingers, something changes. You're still standing in the same room but you've been joined by two familiar figures. Curator Doddwhistle is discussing something with Rigmarole, but their words are impossible to hear. The Cookie Dough bowl has been knocked over.

You read the words *COULD IT BE CORRUPT COPPERS?* in the dough just before Curator Doddwhistle mops it up. You have no idea if she saw the words too.

All around you can hear rushing, whooshing sounds.

"You cannot be seen by those in this vision as you are hidden within the tides of time," says a voice. "I am Bernard the time-bending lobster."

You feel dizzy and confused. You can smell seafood. Is this the future or the past? Or is it a different version of the present?

"There are many seas in time's ocean. You must decide in which you will swim."

This feels more like drowning than swimming. You struggle to breathe. You can feel your body going rigid with panic. Other voices fill your head. They speak over one another, making it impossible to work out who's saying what.

"I literally had time on my hands."

"You're making it sound worse than it is. I would have seen the sponge returned to its rightful owner."

"You won't tell, will you? You and me go way back."

"Bernard the time-bending lobster can be summoned by tearing a page in the book that he wrote."

Bernard's voice floats over the others. "The lamp endlessly slides between the past, present and future. These voices have floated from possible futures. All are possible but only one is inevitable."

You're still trying to make sense of this comment when the voice vanishes and you release your grip on the lamp. The strangeness melts away and you're back in the exhibit room in the present. You stagger and knock the cookie-dough bowl off its stand. It clatters to the ground.

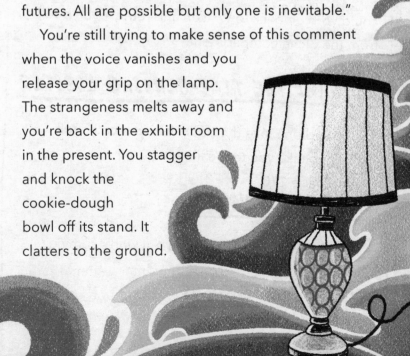

You're so confused but the words that stick with you are those that tell you how to use the book. It's tempting because you still have many questions about the time-bending lobster. You don't know what to think and you're still staring at the spilled dough, watching the words materialize when you hear footsteps. Someone's coming. Should you hide or run? And if you run, what next?

? If you stole the book when you had the chance, you could you run back to Watson and retrieve the book from the glove compartment.

Turn to page 137
BERNARD THE TIME-BENDING LOBSTER

? If you didn't take the book then you could tell Watson to take you to the library.

Turn to page 170
DROUBLE TROUBLE

? Or should you hide and find out who's coming?

Turn to page 162
MARKETING GENIUS

THE END?

"**Most species cannot cope with** the limitless possibilities of life."

The world around you has frozen. Everything is paused. No one moves. Nothing happens. There isn't even a breeze. But it's not silent. Instead, your ears are filled with an endless hum as every noise is elongated.

A floating lobster materializes in front of you. Long antennae drift with the movement of invisible waves. Its six legs wriggle. Its two large claws open and snap shut again. It floats mid-air, untroubled by the normal laws of gravity.

"I am Bernard ... the time-bending lobster," he proclaims grandly.

The more you stare at this bizarre floating crustacean, the more you realize that everything else is falling away. It's the strangest thing. The walls crumble. The floor vanishes. The sky unfurls, like a giant orange being peeled. Klaus and the others drift into the dark ocean that now surrounds you.

It's like a dream.

"These are the tides of time," says Bernard. "You have succeeded. You have recovered the Time Sponge. I am in your debt."

You're in the centre of an enormous bubble suspended in the dark waters that swirl all around. In the shadows, creatures lurk. You feel strangely relaxed as you gaze at the lobster. A question forms in your head.

"You wish to understand why I would hire a detective to find something when I knew who had taken it," says Bernard, reading your thoughts. "If you look inside yourself, you will realize you already know the answer to that question."

It's true. You do understand why he needed to hire Klaus. If he hadn't hired Klaus in the past, the answer would never have been found in the future. That future is now in your past, but you still have a nagging suspicion that things could have turned out differently.

"The Time Sponge in your hand has frozen all of time in your universe but I can help you see through the cracks in reality and show you every possible version of events."

Three specks of light appear in the gloom. Behind each speck is a large dark shadow. As they get closer, you see that the lights are attached to stalks belonging to weird-looking fish with rows of jagged teeth.

"These are time's anglerfish," says Bernard. "Each one represents a point to which you can return. Do you want to see how things could have been? Or perhaps you are satisfied with this ending. One solution is enough for some. They prefer to trudge forwards with their ordinary lives. They fail to see how many possibilities life can offer if you only have the courage to look."

each one is in fact a frozen moment in time. You see Klaus sitting in the car, about to tell you to get in. You see Professor O'Leary standing outside the library. The third shows Klaus entering the police station.

"Most mortals believe that life is a series of choices. Doors open and close. Bridges can be burned. We live with the consequences of our actions. But life is much bigger than that. In truth, the possibilities are endless. How will you choose to go forwards?"

HAVENTRY'S OTHE
LIBRARY

? Do you want to restart at the beginning and find an alternative solution?

Turn to page 11
THE TIME SPONGE

? Or go back to the library visit?

Turn to page 81
HAVENTRY'S OTHER LIBRARY

? Or return to the police station?

Turn to page 127
HANDCUFFS AND ACCUSATIONS

? Or do you want to call it a day and wait for your next mystery to solve?

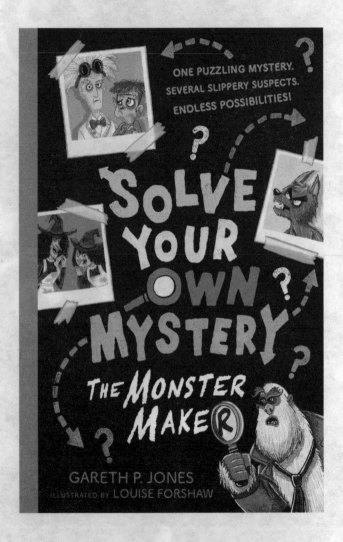